THE
NOMINATIVE
CASE

The Nominative Case

Edward Mackin

Walker and Company
New York

First published in the United States of America in 1991
by Walker Publishing Company, Inc.
Published simultaneously in Canada by Thomas Allen & Son
Canada, Limited, Markham, Ontario

Library of Congress Cataloging-in-Publication Data

Mackin, Edward, 1929–
The nominative case / Edward Mackin.
        p.   cm.
    ISBN 0-8027-5780-4
        I. Title.
PS3563.A31166N58   1991
813'.54—dc20   90-19598
                    CIP

Printed in the United States of America
2 4 6 8 10 9 7 5 3 1

PART ONE

▽

Naming a Chair

$\triangledown$

1

AUGUST FRYE RETURNED FROM class to find young Bledsoe weeping at his desk. Stanley sat bolt upright, corduroy jacket buttoned across his narrow chest, hands flat on the envelope before him, tears streaming from his pinkish eyes and down the plump protrusions of his cheeks. This was the first surprise.

The second surprise was finding that he did not enjoy the sight of Bledsoe in this fallen condition. To see the young man crushed and wailing must have been high among his subconscious desires, but the actual fact of it was, well, embarrassing. August stepped backward to leave their common office.

"Wait! Don't go!"

He hesitated. On the one hand, Bledsoe was arguably a fellow human being. On the other, his peremptory tone brought back Frye's usual dislike for the young pup.

Bledsoe was standing now. He wiped his eyes, and his thin mouth widened into a smile. Tears of gladness?

"Look at this," Bledsoe cried, standing and thrusting the envelope at his office mate.

The envelope contained a letter from the editor of the literary quarterly *Nor'easter* informing Bledsoe that his recently submitted poem had been accepted for publication. A

P.S. identified the poem by its title. Frye looked closely at his junior colleague.

"Well, well."

Bledsoe took the letter and pressed it to his chest. He wore a foolish smile, knew that it was foolish, and did not care.

"A poem! I will be a published poet, August. Nothing else I've done means anything compared with this. Articles?" He dismissed them with a wave of his hand. "I have always thought of myself as primarily a poet."

"I know."

A wary glance. "Did you tell anyone?"

"Tell them what?" Dear God, the vulnerability of the man. Bledsoe exuded articles on nineteenth-century fiction, British and American; he had a book contract to gather an anthology of critical interpretations of George Meredith; he was the least gifted and most published member of the department. Contempt had come hard when Frye realized Bledsoe despised his own output.

"Hackwork. It got me tenure. It will get me full." He meant full professor. "It's all shit."

Frye had nodded. This confession came last April when an unseasonable snowstorm stranded them in the office. Bledsoe had put on his Mr. Coffee and brought junk food from the mechanical vendors in the basement of the building. It became almost cozy with the snow falling outside, Mr. Coffee aglow, August Frye trying to eat a Snickers bar while keeping his lower plate anchored. He found it difficult to chew with a finger in his mouth. It was a moment for confidence.

"They're false?" Bledsoe said.

"Oh, they're real enough. They're just not mine."

Long limbed, high hipped, sandy haired, Bledsoe looked a figure of fun, and was, but mainly he was a pain in the ass.

"I write poetry," Bledsoe had confessed shortly after midnight.

"You'll get over it."

"It's what I really want to do."

"Have you been published?"

"Not since freshman year of college." He sounded as if he might name the day, the month, the year. "In *The Cayugan*." The campus paper at Ithaca College, not Cornell. "I mail off on the average a poem a week."

Dear God.

"That worked with articles."

"Don't give up."

"Give up?"

Inevitably he had shown some of his work to Frye, winning, without need of Frye's assistance, the argument he seemed to be having with himself. Of course, these were not yet finished. Rewriting was the key, didn't Frye think?

"Refried beans are best," Frye agreed. There seemed no way out of this.

Bledsoe had hovered over him as he read the typed pages. Perhaps under other circumstances they would have seemed less awful.

"What do you think?"

"My judgment of poetry is worthless."

"C'mon. You've been teaching . . . what, thirty years?"

"Let me take these and read them again."

Bledsoe nodded at this promise of a considered appraisal. "That's okay. They're on the computer."

Frye had never doubted it. He wrote a page of comment on the poems, a study in obfuscation, half-praise coated with unintelligibility. He had hooted over Stanley's poems with Larry Gridiron and written a parody of them.

"It's better than his," Larry said, spoiling the moment. And now, in September, a tearful Bledsoe gripped a letter of acceptance.

"Which poem was it?"

"I don't know! Isn't that crazy? I have so many out, I don't know which one he had."

"It says 'Fronds.' "

A goofy grin. "I can't remember."

"You can look it up on your computer."

"Ha. Didn't I tell you? My hard disk cracked. God knows what I lost." He hesitated. "The only copy of that poem may be the one at the magazine."

With Bledsoe sobbing and sighing in triumph behind him, Frye sat at his desk and checked his mail. A letter from the dean. He turned to the poet.

"Did you read Maggie's letter?"

Bledsoe nodded. "I read it and then noticed the return address of this. . . . " He actually kissed the letter from the *Nor'easter*. He leaned toward Frye. "You're my candidate."

"Don't you dare!"

"I'm naming you, August. It's about time you were chair."

"I don't want to be chair or table or footstool to the dean. I mean it. How about yourself?"

"Me!"

A poet as chairman of the department? Bledsoe would have leapt at the chance an hour before, but now he found it sacrilegious. But then a speculative look came into his eye.

There was the sound of approaching voices. Bledsoe leaned forward and clutched Frye's arm.

"Not a word," he whispered.

Frye locked his lips and threw away the key.

$\triangledown$

2

NEXT TO THE NOW vacant departmental office was a room called the lounge whose bareness was not much diminished by a Naugahyde couch, nine canvas chairs, a coffee urn, and a rack filled with dog-eared issues of journals in which the staff aspired to appear, bellwethers of the profession. On the wall a print of Melville brooded over the room. In a corner on a straight-back chair sat Wilma Trout, one arm across her little potbelly, hand supporting the elbow of the other arm, which held a book before her pinched peering face. She looked over her reading glasses at the trio of youngsters who had wandered in and sighed.

"The urn is empty," Wilma said.

Quinlan held out an arm, stopping his companions. He seemed to be searching for something on the ceiling. "The urn is empty," he said, testing the line.

"The urn is empty," repeated his companions.

Wilma moved her elbow as if shifting gears and brought her book closer to her face. *Robert Elsmere*. Mrs. Humphrey Ward, London, 1888. Wilma was interested in very little that had been published after that date. She ignored the chanting of her demented junior colleagues, swaying and waving their arms now. *The urn is empty*.

Irene Cossette turned the handle of the coffee urn on and

off in a suggestive way as she chanted, her behemoth bottom swaying with the effort. Quinlan, grinning like an advertisement for Aer Lingus, brought now one knee, now the other, under his chin where a tuft of red hair sought to firm that recessive feature, repeating the incantatory line with closed eyes. The ineffable Bledsoe took a letter from one pocket and put it in another. Wilma rose and followed her book out of the room.

She drifted down the hall to where the door of August Frye's office stood open.

"Is that a prayer service I hear?" August said, closing a desk drawer hastily. Even this late in the day, his after-shave lotion was quite noticeable. Perhaps he had just freshened up.

Wilma rolled her eyes. "Did you receive the dean's letter?"

"Sit down, Wilma. Coffee?"

"Do you have some?"

He pushed back, got up, and crossed the room to where a coffee maker stood on a shelf stuffed with the paperback science fiction on which Bledsoe yearly offered a course. Dear August returned with coffee in a chipped though china cup. Wilma abhorred Styrofoam and did not doubt that one day it would, like asbestos, be identified as the cause of much that is wrong in the modern world.

"The coffee is hot enough to sterilize that cup."

Wilma turned the cup and sipped from the opposite side. There are many rare and exotic diseases 'twixt cup and lip. August nodded in approval.

"They say you can't catch it that way."

Wilma ignored him. "I've been remembering when Lawrence was chairman." She resolutely refused to use the ideological "chairperson" or the noncommittal "chair."

"Ah, yes."

"I have calculated that he left office fifteen years ago."

"That long?"

"Leaving office is a grand way to put it, of course. Things were much simpler even so short a time ago."

August nodded. Wilma rather liked the smell of his lotion. She rather liked August, for that matter. Once she had had a vivid dream in which he wrestled her down on the Naugahyde couch in the lounge.

"Will you support me, August?"

"For chair?"

"Good heavens, no." Imagine having to deal in the line of duty with such creatures as the three she had just left in the lounge. "I think it is time Lawrence Gridiron returned to the helm. We could nominate him together."

"Have you spoken to him?"

"Would that be wise?"

August looked pensive. Wilma thought of August's face as full rather than fat. His head was nicely domed, negating the negative effect of the baldness.

"It's not impossible."

"*Negatio negationis*," she murmured. August stared.

"You're not drinking, August."

"Oh, it's much too early in the day."

"I drink coffee from morning to night."

"What was that you said?"

"A medieval phrase. To say God is not a body is negatively true; negating the negative mimics the positive, as if one could know."

"I see."

"And I see that you don't. I was commenting on your remark that Larry is not unthinkable."

"Ah. Maybe I will have some coffee."

Wilma turned on her meatless shanks and followed him with her eyes. He found an acceptable mug and half filled it with coffee. Back at his desk, he opened a drawer and produced a bottle.

"Care for a little?"

"What is it?"

He looked at the label. "Brandy. I confiscated it from Bledsoe."

"How can you stand to share an office with that man?"

"It was him or Quinlan."

"Hobson's choice."

"You haven't spoken to Maggie about Gridiron?"

"I wanted to consult you first."

"Tell her. It's time we brought Larry out of retirement."

August's little joke, of course. Larry Gridiron was a year younger than Wilma, and Wilma had no intention of retiring, ever. The thought of making room for another like the three she had just left in the lounge sickened her. She held out her cup.

"Let me have some brandy."

He poured a dollop into her coffee, then put the bottle away. Wilma sniffed her cup.

"It smells like after-shave lotion."

"Wait'll you taste it."

▽

3

AFTER WILMA TROUT LEFT the lounge Quinlan collapsed on the couch, causing it to give off a prolonged sigh, and Irene Cossette eased herself onto a canvas chair. At the magazine rack, Bledsoe stood observing his prosaic colleagues.

"Who're you going to push for chair?" he asked.

Irene looked at Quinlan. "Who would want the job?"

Bledsoe smiled. Irene would join Weight Watchers for a chance at the job. He said, "Poor old Frye all but begged me not to nominate him."

"Frye," Irene said in a neutral tone. Perhaps she thought Bledsoe favored Frye.

"Frye wouldn't be so bad," Quinlan said. "He's full of shit, but he's always been nice enough to me."

"You didn't want to be his office mate."

"That's true."

Bledsoe looked at Melville on the wall and resolved to read "Clarel," the interminable poem Herman had written in his old age. One noontime with Larry Gridiron, Bledsoe had visited the site of the house in which Melville had died.

"Ever read his poetry?" Larry had asked.

"Just the stuff in the *Portable Melville*."

"It's all that bad."

"I kind of liked some of it."

11

"He should have stuck with sailors and the South Seas."

"You may be right."

"Look at *Billy Budd.*"

Now with the letter of acceptance in an inside pocket, pressed to his rib cage, Bledsoe shared a smile of complicity with Melville. If only he could remember the poem that had been accepted. He imagined writing the editor and asking to see a copy of his own poem. Just say he hadn't kept a copy? That would sound too casual, as if he really didn't care. An idea caused him to push away from the magazine rack. It rocked against the wall and then outward. It teetered again and fell. Irene screamed, and the canvas chair crumpled beneath her just as the magazine rack crashed down, catching the back of Bledsoe's heel. His fall was broken by the plump bulk of Irene.

"Glory be to God," Quinlan cried.

"Amen," Larry Gridiron said, coming into the lounge and taking hold of the fallen rack. "Give me a hand, Quinlan."

Quinlan, the bastard, began to applaud.

"Help me lift this!" Gridiron barked.

The pain started then, belatedly, in Bledsoe's heel. How warm Irene's breasts were. She was holding him tightly. Gridiron and Quinlan got the rack off his heel. The pain seemed to increase.

"I think it's broken."

"I can't get up," Irene said.

Gridiron looked down at the fallen maiden cradling the felled Bledsoe. Lifting the magazine rack was one thing; Irene was definitely another. He took her hand, and Quinlan took the other.

"Get off her, Bledsoe."

Others were entering the lounge. Bledsoe was alerted to this by Irene's girlish giggle. Stella Houston glared down at him. Information about rape prevention with hot line numbers was featured on the little bulletin board on her office door. "Sex Is Rape." This enigmatic slogan headlined the board. Coeds regularly complained of Stella's advances.

Bledsoe felt he was proving one of her theories. He got off Irene and tried to stand. His foot would not support him. Stella gave him a shove, and he staggered toward the couch. Meanwhile, Irene was raised to her feet and a chair was brought forward.

"Not another canvas one," Quinlan advised.

Irene was the center of attention. Bledsoe remembered what he had been thinking when he pushed away from the rack. Frye might have a copy of the accepted poem. He hadn't returned the sheaf Bledsoe had pressed upon him last spring. Bledsoe couldn't remember whether he had mailed the poem before or since then. But a wait of a year before a rejection arrived was not unusual. Frye had to have it.

He pushed his way through the crowd around Irene and hobbled down the hall, Oedipus the lame.

At the sight of Wilma sitting in the office with Frye, Bledsoe went on to the men's room. His heel was killing him.

▽

4

"WHAT I WOULD like . . . ," Wilma said, her voice and eyes dropping. But she shook her head violently, as if to repress the desire. "No."

Bledsoe hobbled past the open door for the second time, looking furtively in but going on. Being polite? August Frye doubted it. It would never dawn on Bledsoe that he could interrupt anything more important than his own entry into a room.

"What would you like?" he asked Wilma. "And don't be nasty."

"Oh, August."

At what age does one stop blushing? August wondered when he himself had last blushed. But he could wonder how long it had been since he'd done a number of things.

"Tell me."

"It's silly, I know that. You remember what Boethius says about those who seek happiness in honors."

"Being chair isn't much of an honor, Wilma."

"I do not want to be chairman of this department." She spoke very precisely, lingering on each word, meaning them separately and collectively. Frye believed her.

"What honor tempts you?"

14

"That." She pointed to a framed letter behind Bledsoe's desk. English Teacher of the Year.

"Wilma!"

The blush was even bloodier this time. "I know. I know. I said it was silly. But I want it!"

The Teacher of the Year Award was a device used to cushion a decision against promotion or to sweeten a less-than-average raise. It voided the phrase *"honoris causa"* of what little meaning thousands of commencements had left it. The award was named after Olive Pettigrew Green, who had been the first professor of English when the Lyndon Johnson campus of the City University of New York had opened. Olive was sixty at the time, and she retired five years later. At sixty-nine, she and her sister were arrested at the Tijuana border trying to smuggle Laetrile into the States. Her impassioned plea, in which she claimed a constitutional right to buy and use any medication she wanted—it was why she had fought in the war, as a WAAC—gained her a brief moment in the media sun. At an endless and boring meeting, August had suggested the inauguration of a teacher award in honor of Olive. The motion carried, of course. Once or twice since, when vindictive colleagues tried to make him the Olive Pettigrew Green Teacher of the Year, August had pleaded conflict of interest and been spared. Bledsoe was honored at last May's commencement.

"This makes it all worthwhile," August had said when the impending award became known in April.

"Why, thank you."

"At the time the award was conceived, it was precisely someone like yourself we had in mind."

Bledsoe had frowned away his smile. "They're not going to consider me for promotion to full this year."

Didn't he see the connection between that and the award?

"You'd think this would put me over the top, wouldn't you?"

"Let's just say it puts you on top."

"Wilma," August said now, "I'll make a deal with you."

Her eyes widened as if she thought he might say something nasty.

"I'll put you up for the Olive Pettigrew Green if you don't put me up for chair."

"But that's not fair."

"I know. But you want the damned thing."

Wilma stood and leaned toward the framed document signed by George Blair, the chair, and Maggie and Gregory Hackis, the college president, informing Bledsoe and all to whom these presents came of the bestowal of this signal honor. Are there unsignaled honors?

Bledsoe came along again, hesitated in the doorway, pointed at Wilma, and made an elaborate gesture, an umpire declaring a batter out.

"I was just admiring your award," Wilma said, her nose still within reach of the framed letter. The glass acted as enough of a mirror for her to make out Bledsoe in the doorway.

Bledsoe limped in. What else could he do? "You've received it yourself, I suppose."

"Stanley," Frye said, "you have just stumbled upon the skeleton in the departmental closet. Wilma has never been so honored. It is high time she was named Teacher of the Year, don't you agree?"

Bledsoe slipped around his desk and dropped into his chair, nodding all the while. "I do."

"We'll write a joint letter," Frye promised.

Wilma, flustered to have her ambition so much in the public domain, started for the door.

"What do you think of August as chair?" Bledsoe called after her.

She turned in the doorway, glanced at August, and shook her head. And then she was gone.

"Ungrateful bitch," Bledsoe said.

"Why were you cruising the hallway?"

"August, that poem. It's driving me crazy. Is there any possibility you would have a copy of the poems I gave you?"

"I'll check tonight."

" 'Fronds.' "

"I remember."

Bledsoe relaxed, sliding down in his chair, closing his eyes. "I should have asked Wilma to put me up for chair."

"Surprise, Stanley. That is what she means to do."

His eyes popped open. "Really?"

"There's still time to stop her."

That was cruel. But then, it had been far more cruel to concoct a sort of lampoon of Bledsoe's verse and submit it for publication as one of Stanley's own.

"My heel is giving me intense pain."

"Is that an ambulance siren I hear? Maybe it's come for you."

5

DEAN MAGGIE DOWNS STARED at the roster of the English Department as her aunt Ida had once stared at tea leaves, but all she saw was what she saw. Such a collection of mediocrities! For two years she had fought with Blair, but now she almost wished he were still alive. A known evil.

Trout, Gridiron, Quinlan, Houston, Harsch, Goldwyn, Bledsoe, Weinstein, Frye—these, plus two more on leave, Morris and Slattery—were the tenured members. Below them were lower forms of academic life, some on tenure tracks, others part of that pool of exploitable personnel to be found in the vicinity of any college, the casualties of the system who nonetheless had credentials, could not turn their backs definitively on the classroom and so were vulnerable to offers of annual contracts, piecework. As a whole, the department was the sum of its parts.

"Three replies to your letter," Haddock said, dropping them on her desk and turning to go. Her assistant dean was a riot of mismatched clothing—glen plaid jacket, striped slacks, saddle shoes, a paisley print tie making the neck of his polo shirt look like a sachet bag.

"Wait." She pushed the letters aside. The letter to the English faculty was *pro forma*. What did she care who they wanted. Whom? She asked Haddock.

"Whom." He might be right. He wasn't in English.

"They don't want anyone rocking the boat," she said.

"Neither do you."

"That's true. I don't want another Blair." She looked up. "Sorry." Haddock and Blair had been in the same weekly poker game.

"I think of him as retired."

It had the sound of an epitaph, almost touching. Maggie sat back. Haddock was crude but efficient, and he kept the students from her door. He was worth his weight in gold and grossly underpaid. And he was touchingly devoted to her, gender speaking faintly to gender beneath the daily business of the dean's office. She half hoped Haddock's manner with her would divert attention from her and Greg Hackis.

Haddock said, "Someone nominated Wilma Trout."

"Someone?"

"Anonymous."

Maggie found the letter. "That's Wilma's handwriting."

"It's typed."

"Then there are two votes for Wilma."

"Strange," Haddock said. "I thought she was well liked. The kids like her."

"B+ Wilma. Of course they like her."

"B+ is the average grade in the college."

"Name some of the previous chairpersons."

"Gridiron was the best."

Another of his poker pals. "Too old."

"There's Bledsoe."

He was getting back at her, about Blair, about Gridiron.

"You know what's going to have to be done."

Haddock nodded. He never sat down when he came into her office. She liked it that he was so formal with her; it kept things completely professional. Did he enjoy subservience to her? Whatever, Haddock was the only one in the college she trusted. Their relationship was like an arranged marriage.

"Pick some tough bitch," he said.

"Not on your life." One was enough. She wanted weak-

ness, not strength, in the next English chair, who would have
to preside over the elimination of three positions. It would
have been four if Blair hadn't died. "What do you think of
August Frye?"

"He wouldn't take it."

"Why not?"

"Why should he?"

Prestige? Money? Power? August Frye was Maggie's
choice, and she meant to have him.

"You're probably right."

A siren seemed to have stopped in the street just below.
Haddock went to the window. "An ambulance."

It had been called for Irene Cossette, who'd had some kind
of accident in the English lounge. When Maggie arrived, she
found that Stella Houston had put herself in charge and was
shouting orders at the paramedics, who blanched at the size
of Irene. The felled professor lay on the floor like a grounded
dirigible.

Stella came up to Maggie. "I am going to encourage her to
sue."

"Be careful."

"Is that a threat?"

"I don't want you arrested for practicing law without a
license."

"A citizen's arrest?"

"The objective, not the possessive genitive," an unmis-
takable voice said, and Maggie turned to face August Frye.
"Maybe they should lower her out of a window."

Having lifted Irene, the paramedics stood indecisively.
Even without the dean in it, the door would be a tight
squeeze.

"That woman is injured," Stella said in shocked tones.

"I was thinking of the Acts of the Apostles," August said
sweetly.

"I'll bet you were."

Maggie liked the way August handled Stella Houston. He
was saying something about a paralytic and Paul and a hole

in the ceiling—incomprehensible, but what did it matter? He would be perfect as chair of English. Not malleable, perhaps, but that was a two way street. Blair had been tough with her and soft with the faculty. Frye would be uniformly intransigent.

Two more letters had arrived when she went back to her office. Not a single vote for August Frye. But the faculty was the cabinet; she was Lincoln. The analogy limped, like Bledsoe. Hackis was president, not she. But Maggie's was the only vote that counted with him.

$\triangledown$

6

" 'Fronds?'' LARRY GRIDIRON said. He and August were dining in the Guillotine in the Village, where the drinks were served in balloon glasses.

"We were drunk at the time."

"Funny I don't remember."

As it happened, Larry remembered the occasion all too well. He did not propose to discuss the matter until they were in the condition they had been in when they colluded on "Fronds," particularly because there was a vestigial trace of remorse in August's eye.

"You have to remember. I wrote it out at a table in the White Horse."

When he was with August, Larry ordered manhattans too. Sweet vermouth was a little cloying, but the musky taste had pleasant associations. An evening with August was always memorable, often because he couldn't remember a thing afterward. Twice he had greeted the dawn in a Hoboken hotel.

"Halfway across, my legs began to cramp," August said, "so I turned back."

"C'mon. I don't know how to swim."

"You learned fast. Of course, we had no choice."

He knew his leg was being pulled. More likely than not,

August had put him in a cab and paid the cabby to book him into the hotel. But twice?

"Don't tell me I swam," he said the second time.

"Swim? She would have floated."

"She?"

No wonder he hated August. On any objective estimate, Gridiron assured himself, he outshone his old nemesis. He had made full professor first, he had published two and a half books—co-editing an anthology of novellas—he was the more popular teacher, he was better looking than the plump, bald Frye. Why was August better liked?

There was only one answer. August was the major butt of his own jokes. Self-effacement as preemptive strike. He could have been chairman any time he said so, he could have had the goddam Olive Pettigrew Green award, he could have been assistant dean.

"You're too proud, August."

"I know. I have this hunger for advancement and reward."

"You'd rather sneer at them. That's how you adjust to failure."

"By succeeding at it?"

"You know what I mean."

"That would make one of us."

That son of a bitch. Well, this time he was outgunned. Larry had it straight from Haddock.

"Maggie's going to name August," Haddock had said. He sniffed before and after speaking, a nervous habit picked up at poker.

"He agreed?"

"She's going to draft him."

"He'll refuse."

"On what grounds?"

"There's nothing in his contract says he's got to accept the chairmanship."

Haddock had smiled. "He won't know what hit him."

"Anything I can do?" Larry fanned his cards. Four hearts. "It's about time something happened to August."

"Yeah."

He got a club on the draw, which gave him a pair of tens, and Haddock raked in the pot on the basis of openers.

Maybe Frye was in on it and that's why Haddock had been so smug. Gridiron simply could not tell. It was like having enemies as well as paranoia, the liar's paradox, or what August had just called the no-cal iced tea on the menu. *Negatio negationis.*

"What's it mean?"

"Ask Wilma."

"Ask her what?"

August sipped his second jumbo-sized manhattan, peering at Gridiron. He put his glass down carefully.

" 'These palms no fingers sprout,' " he said dreamily.

" 'But green-fleshed raise a doubt,' " Gridiron added.

"Go on, go on."

He was further along in his second drink than August, but he picked up his glass anyway. "That's all I remember."

August drew a folded piece of paper from his shirt pocket and tapped it against his forehead.

"I thought you sent it in."

"This is the one I submitted in Stanley's name. I retained the title 'Fronds.' "

"Bledsoe thinks he wrote it?"

"He writes so many poems, he doesn't remember half of them. That he doesn't have a copy is no surprise. His computer suffered a breakdown."

"Let me see it."

"Not while we're eating."

Sirloin strip, tossed salad, no potato, a third manhattan. What Larry had to fight against was the sense of camaraderie, good fellowship; two old farts out on the town, wanting nothing more than a good meal and too much to drink. August Frye was not what he appeared. Maybe nobody was, but like everyone else Gridiron had always considered August an exception, just what he seemed. That was before Bledsoe moved into an office with him.

"What did you ever do to August Frye?" Bledsoe had asked a few weeks later.

"How so?"

"I always thought you were friends."

"That son of a bitch?" Gridiron had been kidding.

"So it's mutual."

Bledsoe. He dismissed it. Or tried to. He waited for Bledsoe to bring it up again. Sought him out in the lounge, happened to be passing the room when Bledsoe's class let out, but the scrawny shit just would not mention August. Finally, Larry asked him what he had meant. The August Frye Bledsoe described was a stranger, yet somehow recognizable. Imagine him resenting Larry Gridiron all those years.

Now, having finished his steak, Gridiron took off his trifocals and put on his bottle-bottom glasses, but he still had trouble reading the unfolded sheet. He was drunk. Mildly drunk, but drunk. Just what he'd sworn he wouldn't do. Oh, what the hell. No point going out if you were going to act like a monk. In this condition he regarded August as he always had, his best friend. Imagine August telling those things to Bledsoe, though. Drunk, Larry couldn't imagine it.

"You read it, August."

He did, with feeling. People at other tables looked at them, not annoyed, but smiling approvingly. Gridiron looked like a poet, so they assumed August really was one. Well, August had done "Fronds" by himself, no matter what he said. Drunk or sober, Gridiron could not write a line of verse.

"What a dirty trick," Gridiron said, but thinking of Bledsoe made him laugh.

"I did him a favor. It's his first published poem."

"Only it's not his."

"You can say that again."

"It's not so bad."

"It's Henry VIII."

"Not VII?"

"That's your last drink."

Well, it was the last one he remembered ordering, anyway.

$\triangledown$

7

STELLA HOUSTON STARED ACROSS the desk at the dean with open hostility written all over her leathery face.

"If you really care what we think, Dean Downs, let us elect our new chairperson."

"Who do you think would win?" Maggie asked.

"I have no idea."

"I have. These interviews are a species of ballot, Stella."

"Do you call the male professors by their first names?"

"Would you like me to call you Professor Houston?"

"I would."

"These interviews enable members of your department to express their views quite freely. I can tell you that no one has recommended that you be appointed."

Maggie sat back as she said this, the better to enjoy Stella's discomfiture. Always on her dignity, Stella was constantly being insulted. For the moment she was speechless. Maggie sat forward.

"Yet you may be the best-qualified person for the job. You can see my problem."

To ask Stella to see an administrator's side of an issue was like asking her to use the men's room. Not that Maggie was a male chauvinist. The men were as absurd as Stella. She found it best to think of the faculty as a group of arrested adolescents, confined to the playground for life, resenting grown-ups. The oldest member of the faculty felt more affinity with the rawest freshman than with any ordinary adult.

"This whole process is a charade," Stella managed to say.

"Of course it is. Life is a charade. An election would be a charade."

"It would tell us who the department wants."

"I already know that. One after another of your colleagues has come in here and put the same person's name before me."

"Who?"

"You know who." Whom? Stella's perplexity was not grammatical. She could not admit to being completely unaware of her colleagues' choice, and if she suggested she knew, she was taking part in the charade. But then, to have answered this call for consultation was already to take part. Maggie of course was lying when she said there was a consensus in the department on a new chair. She had no fear of this being discovered. Not that she thought of it as lying. She thought of it as administering.

"Yes, it is who you think," Maggie added, smiling slightly.

"Whom I think? If there is such unanimity, why do you fear an election?"

"I fear what an election would do to the English Department, certainly. You're the only one who has suggested an election."

"Then you haven't spoken to Irene Cossette."

It was a desperate remark, Maggie knew, what the philosophers would call a counterexample. At least it was entertaining to fence verbally with the antic types in the philosophy department. For them life was a game anyway, and one they were prepared to lose. Alas for Stella, her ruse could not work.

"I have just come from the hospital, where in fact I spoke with Professor Cossette."

"How is she?"

"Unharmed. Not even a bruise. She has promised to take care of the chair."

"The chair! Irene?"

"I mean the one she broke. It must be replaced. It was city property, after all."

"She should sue the city."

"I don't think she is going to take your advice."

"Whom did she nominate?"

"Oh, I would never divulge a confidence. But I can tell you that your colleagues as a group want August Frye in the chair."

It was interesting to see how members of the English Department reacted to this false claim, to watch well up in their eyes the image of a solid majority lined up behind August. The last thing an academic wanted was to be isolated from the herd. Stella nodded with noncommittal thoughtfulness.

"He'd never accept."

"It is my experience that faculty usually accept opportunities offered to them."

"Not August." A snitcher's look came over Stella's face. "He despises Lyndon Johnson," she said. "He despises the school, its students, you, all of us."

"In short, he's a typical member of the faculty."

"That's not true. I love teaching."

Poor Stella. How she wanted to be a pied piperette after whom hordes of docile youngsters marched onward to wherever she was going. It was easy to find what Stella did not like, but the ideal she put before the young was the rejection of the status quo, the establishment, the smug middle-class mentality that was suffocating the country. Products of the ghetto did not respond to this message from a member of the smug middle class. The only course of Stella's that was a draw was George Eliot's Women, and that was because it was touted by the Gay/Lesbian Coalition. The militancy of that organization was a mixed blessing for Stella, who belonged to a generation that considered discretion the better part of valor.

The interview ended with Stella making a formal request for the election of the new chair of English.

"I will act on it as soon as possible."

"Act on it now."

"Very well. I deny your request."

"Women should stick together, Maggie."

"Just what I was going to say to you, Professor Houston."

$\triangledown$

8

AFTER DINNER THE NIGHT before, he and Larry had gone to the Garden for fights in the Felt Forum.

"It answers a felt need, Larry."

The tickets they bought from the scalper outside were indeed ringside, and they spent several hours being sprayed with sweat and blood. A huge black man next to Larry was smoking a vile cigar. He wore a pin he insisted they read. "Thank you for not smoking: it leaves more for me." August read it aloud, knowing Larry could barely see.

"I can barely see, said the nudist."

Wit was wasted on Larry by that point. The evening had been disappointing so far as "Fronds" was concerned. August had anticipated a delightful exchange, laughter, hooting at the idiocy of their junior colleague. Not much of that had been forthcoming. Larry had difficulty, or said he did, remembering the night they had mailed off the poem. But then August had stretched it a bit, saying they had written the one he had submitted in Stanley's name. Copied it would have been more accurate.

It occurred to him then that Larry had changed over the past year. Was he ill? To think it was to believe it. Larry looked well, of course, but wasn't that one of the first signs? His eyes were going, he couldn't hold liquor, and his memory was shot. Alzheimer's? Naw. Just ordinary senility. But the wary expression, the holding back when they were supposedly on the town, suggested worse.

"You see your doctor lately?"

Larry nodded. He hadn't understood. It wasn't just the noise level in the Forum; Larry's ears were going too. The son of a bitch had all his teeth and hair, though. He would look good at the wake. August didn't find that at all funny. Blair's death had been a blow. Blair had been two years younger than August Frye, three years younger than Larry. It had been Blair's heart. There hadn't been a death for three years, and then, whammo. The cleaning crew found Blair sitting at his desk, dead as a mackerel. The first since Spritzer the medievalist. Leukemia. God. Young Jones had gone away with AIDS, but he was only a one-year replacement. The thought that Larry Gridiron had a terminal illness grew on August through the evening. He took Larry home in a cab, told the driver to wait until he was safely inside.

"Whatsa matter, he drunk?"

"Drunk? Don't you know who that is?"

"Who?"

"Mayor Koch."

That shut him up. August studied the man's license. Iranian? New York had become a Third World city. Last summer he had told a woman driver, a Puerto Rican, "Take me to the Algonquin." She looked it up in her book. Under G. The El Gonquin?

Now today in the office August imagined that he knew Larry was ill, as if his old friend had confided in him. *August, I'm dying.* The scene was vivid because he had dreamt it. It woke him up and he couldn't get back to sleep, and now he had a headache. Only a headache. He should thank God. Poor Larry. He said it aloud.

Bledsoe had hobbled in ten minutes before, hardly breaking August's reverie.

"Poor Larry how?"

August started at the sound of Bledsoe's voice, as if

surprised the young man was at his desk. "It's a long story."

"You guys have a fight or what?"

"How do you mean?"

"What's he got against you?"

"The list is endless."

"Well, if it doesn't bother you."

August tried to resist. Already Bledsoe had the deviousness of a dean. He would go places in the academic world, no doubt about it. "Tell me, Stanley."

"Not on your life. The bearer of bad news is bad news."

"He's ill, Stanley. Mortally ill. He's withdrawing into himself."

"What's he got?"

August displayed a palm. Which reminded him of "Fronds." He handed Bledsoe a piece of paper.

"There's your poem."

Bledsoe snatched it from him eagerly and devoured it with his eyes, a smile coming and going on his thin lips, trying to see the poem as the millions of its readers would. He put it down, looking thoughtful.

"Why did I call it 'Fronds'?"

"I wondered about that myself."

He couldn't make it look like a computer printout, but he had typed it out an hour before, using Bledsoe's Selectric. He made a photocopy in Haddock's office and slipped the original into the drawer with his brandy. He had come upon the poem, attributed to Henry VIII, in a collection of medieval English lyrics. He modernized the spelling and supplied the title.

> Green grows the holly
> So does the ivy.
> Though winter blasts never so high,
> Green grows the holly.
>
> As the holly grows green
> And never changes hue
> So am I and ever have been
> To my lady true.

There was more, but he had been in a hurry. In the White Horse he had made a more careful copy, having gained Gridiron's complicity, and sent it off as a contribution from Stanley Bledsoe, Department of English, Lyndon Johnson Community College, New York City.

"I should have called it 'Holly'," Bledsoe said.

"You can still change it."

"You like 'Holly'?"

"Only when it's green."

"August, about Gridiron."

"Yes?"

"How about putting him up for chair?"

"Have you talked with Maggie yet?"

"In fifteen minutes."

"There's your chance."

Stanley nodded; his thoughts were drifting. "Do you think I should mention the acceptance of the poem?"

A little twinge of conscience made August Frye hesitate, but only for a moment.

"Great idea."

▽

9

"DOES IT REALLY matter?" Bledsoe asked when the dean put the question to him. His manner was arch and above the fray, and the look in his eyes was otherworldly, as if some muse might imminently speak in his ear.

"To me or to you?"

"Maybe if Blair hadn't died I would have been put up for promotion to full."

"You got the Olive Pettigrew Green award, didn't you?"

"I've just had a poem accepted for publication." The words emerged as naturally as an exhalation.

"That's nice."

Nice! Bledsoe could have kicked himself around the office for just blurting it out like that. It was his ace, the last trump, the winning card, and he had just sailed it onto the table as if it were the two of clubs. Moreover, the dean's deflating reaction made clear to him how much weight an accepted poem carried with her. The fact was, it didn't sound like much. Depression settled over him like a lead overcoat.

"Where will it appear?"

"In the *Nor'easter Quarterly*."

"I don't think I know it."

"It's very prestigious." His voice cracked. He sounded as if he were going to cry. Oh God, if he could just crawl out of here.

"I look forward to reading it."

"I'll send you a copy. When it's published."

"About the English chair."

"I don't want the job." These words too just emerged. Some evil demon had taken him over. What might he not say next? But Maggie Downs nodded.

"I'll respect that. What do you think of August Frye?"

"We get along."

"His name keeps coming up."

"For chair? August?" He laughed joylessly. "Not a chance."

"You think he would refuse?"

"I know he would."

"Stanley, I have an idea you could persuade him to take it."

Her remark enabled him to recover a shred of dignity. He considered it thoughtfully. "How?"

"Tell him I am thinking of appointing Larry Gridiron."

Bledsoe shook his head. "Gridiron's ill."

"Ill? What do you mean?"

"All I know is that it's got August very upset. I suppose because of their falling-out."

"What falling-out?"

Bledsoe sighed. "It's a long, dull story."

"Would you like a cup of coffee?"

"Yes!"

"Decaf?"

"Coffee." Decaf indeed. What did she take him for?

For the next half hour he had the dean's undivided attention, and that did something to restore his self-esteem. He would have given much to have held back the announcement of his accepted poem until then. He considered mentioning it again, trying for a self-mocking August Frye approach, but reluctantly decided to let it lie. Maggie Downs was taken completely by surprise in the matter of the mortal illness of Larry Gridiron.

"He looks healthy as a horse."

Stanley considered the dean. Was there a Messalina lurking beneath that pin-striped exterior? Charcoal suit, pink blouse gathered nicely at the throat, single pearl earrings in her lobes, fine thick hair, the eyes of a mugger, and a sarcastic mouth. It was said she lusted after the presidency and the president, in that order. Hackis, the president, was a defeated congressman whose book on his six years in Washington had earned him more notoriety than his political career. His doctorate in hotel management from Cornell had done the rest. He was a shoo-in with the board and became Lyndon Johnson's fifth president at the same time that Maggie ascended to the dean's office from the education department. No doubt she felt that if Hackis could do it, she could too. Thus is political ambition born.

"He does look healthy as a horse."

"What does he have?"

Bledsoe thought about it. He had no desire to give up his advantage by admitting to ignorance now.

"I don't know what kind of cancer it is."

"Cancer!"

"The one grim blessing in all this is that two old friends can reconcile before it is too late."

"August Frye and Larry Gridiron are thick as thieves. They always have been. I've heard nothing . . . "

"Sharing an office with August makes me privy to things I otherwise wouldn't know. I'm not sure it's really ethical for me . . . "

"Nonsense. If one of my faculty is seriously ill, I have a right to know about it." She stared vacantly at the window as if some prankster had just soaped "All Men are Mortal" on it. She would not object to the sexist language of that one. "Poor Larry."

She seemed genuinely moved, if only by the realization that she too must one day, perhaps sooner than she imagined, approach the grim boundary between the quick and the dead. Bledsoe would have liked to write that down, but it had an echoing sound to it. His greatest problem as a poet was to screen out ready-made and remembered phrases.

"August is devastated."

"I don't wonder."

He had passed the lead overcoat to her, and he was enjoying it. At thirty-three, Stanley Bledsoe was still young enough to imagine that a cure for death would be found before it got to him. A presidential task force, billions in the budget, a national TV campaign. If safe sex, why not safe life? He shook his head. Sharing the office with August was taking its toll on his sense of humor.

Maggie sat back, steepled her fingers, and spoke an *ad hoc* eulogy for Larry Gridiron. Stanley was moved. It was all bullshit, of course; Larry as teacher, Larry as colleague, Larry as scholar(!). After a good early start, Gridiron had in the past ten years published three letters to the *Voice*, a book review in the *New Republic* and almost had a story taken by the *New Yorker*.

"We shall all miss him," Maggie concluded, clearly practicing the funeral-parlor oration she would speak over the mortal remains of Larry Gridiron.

When she stood, she thrust her hand across the desk. He took it and had his vigorously shaken.

"Thanks for confiding in me, Stanley. I won't forget it." She paused. "I'd like to see a copy of that poem before it appears, if I may."

Bledsoe's manner was once more buoyant when he left the dean's office.

Haddock, lighting a cigarette, squinted at him. "I was about to call the morals squad. You were in there long enough." Joking, of course, but Haddock was protective of the dean. It was like being quizzed by the brother of the girl you had dated.

"She didn't know about Gridiron," Stanley whispered.

Haddock was momentarily puzzled.

"Deans are always the last to know," he said.

10

HADDOCK RATHER INSISTENTLY ASKED August Frye to come out to Chock Full O'Nuts for a cup of coffee, casting enigmatic glances at Bledsoe, who was brooding over his accepted poem. They went down and out and across the street, and as soon as they were uncomfortable in the molded plastic seats Haddock said, "What's Larry got?"

"You've heard something?"

"Not from Larry."

Haddock said this with mild indignation, as if he should be the first recipient of bad news. Well, he'd had a lot of practice. Widowed twice, the second time when his wife was pushed from a platform under a train, a daughter who appeared regularly on the public access channel talking of her life as a hustler, a career that had crested as assistant dean at Lyndon Johnson.

"Who told you?" August asked.

"Maggie."

"Maggie! Then it is true."

He had some notion that the dean must have received official word. From whom? He wasn't thinking clearly. Sitting across from Haddock sipping coffee that was better than the surroundings, he felt the full impact of the news. Larry terminally ill. His intuitions had been right, as they so often were.

"I'm terminally ill, said the airport manager."

"Have you talked with him about it?" Haddock asked.

"Not in so many words."

Haddock nodded. He understood. What would you say? "About your coming death, Larry . . . "

Larry was younger than he was, the same age as Haddock, yet he could easily imagine outliving them both. Meaning that he could not yet really imagine himself dead. That seemed more of an accomplishment than a defect, as if imagining it increased one's vulnerability. Shirley had been dead for ten years, but August pretended she was visiting her sister in Duluth.

"Larry won last week at poker."

"Good," August said. The conversation continued idiotically, neither knowing quite what to say.

"You know, August. If it was me, I wouldn't have told him either." The thought seemed to brighten Haddock.

"More coffee?"

"It would keep me awake, and I work until five."

"Did Maggie say what it was?" August asked as they were standing halfway across the street, traffic roaring past fore and aft.

"Cancer."

"Dear God."

This ejaculation referred as much to the cab that brushed his arm as commiseration for Larry Gridiron. If they didn't watch out, he and Haddock would be casualties here and now. One should always cross at the corner this time of day.

"It's true about Gridiron," August told Stanley after closing the door of their office.

Stanley nodded but did not look up from his poem. "I might change more than the title of this, August."

"Change it too much and they'll change their minds."

A look of pure terror came over Bledsoe. "Don't say that."

"You've got their letter. You could sue for breach of promise."

Grim faced, Bledsoe nodded. "I told Maggie."

"What did she say?"

"At first, not much, as if it would be infra dig to acknowledge what it means. Has she ever published anything?"

"Deans don't publish."

"They just sit in judgment on those who do."

"Better them than critics."

"Finally she said what she should have said in the first place. For a while I was sorry I mentioned it. Imagine, feeling you should apologize for becoming a published poet."

"Do you have any more in the mail?"

Bledsoe grinned slyly. "I figure strike while the iron is hot. This morning I sent off three more to the *Nor'easter*."

"The next thing you know, you'll be thinking of a volume."

"God, I hope so."

August would feel a lot better about this if Stanley could sell one of his own poems to the quarterly. And to other magazines. The likelihood of this happening seemed slim, however. Stanley's stuff did not have the outrageous ineptitude of the putatively innovative. It was awful in traditional forms. Stanley reached a page toward August.

"Here's one I did last night."

"Last night?"

"I did two others, but this is the best."

August had no choice but to read it.

> The power that pushes into birth
> From earth the flower
> Presses me to thee

He let his eyes skim over three other stanzas without reading them.

"Notice the tricky internal rhymes in the first two lines of each stanza?"

"Very nice."

"You really like it?"

"It reminds me of something."

"Where? What? Look, August, do this for me. Underline

anything that sounds familiar. I don't want to echo other people's stuff."

"Oh, there's nothing like that here."

"It's the bane of teaching literature, isn't it? Our heads are full of so much, it's not easy to sort out whose is whose."

"Did you ever read Henry VIII?"

"Henry VIII?" Stanley half smiled in case this was a joke.

"There are some lyrics ascribed to him."

"So?"

"Nothing." He picked the page up and didn't read it again. He felt he had given Stanley a species of warning in case the editor identified the source of "Fronds." Not likely, he told himself. He had looked at some back issues of the quarterly that Stanley had obligingly provided. That was when he noticed that publication was contingent on ordering a sizable number of copies of the issue in which one's work appeared. It did not seem a journal that would be too concerned about derivative work.

Three thuds sounded on their closed office door, and then it opened. The visitor seemed to duck his head in order to look in. His eye lit on Stanley, and he came in.

"I'm in your novel."

"Yes, yes, I recognize you."

"I gotta pass that course."

He weighed nearly three hundred pounds, he was six and a half feet tall, and his pigmentation was so dark it was clear there had been no miscegenation in his family since they had been brought from Africa. What was someone that size doing at Lyndon Johnson? He should be at a school with a football team, where it would matter less that he was illiterate. Then he wouldn't need to pass a course like Stanley Bledsoe's.

August got up to go. He would leave this scholar alone with his teacher. On his way to the door, he heard Stanley say that the requirements of the course were set forth in the syllabus, and as August closed the door the student repeated more insistently, "I gotta pass this course."

As August pulled the door shut behind him, Larry Gridiron came out of his office across the hall.

"Larry, how are you?"

Gridiron turned, surprised, and August realized it was an odd way to greet a colleague he had seen several times already that day.

▽

11

GRIDIRON HAD NO INTENTION of going out two nights in a row with August Frye. Maxine had given him the silent treatment at breakfast, which, added to the locked bedroom door last night, was pretty stiff punishment seeing that he had after all come home and hadn't spent the night in Hoboken. Not that sleeping on the couch was wholly puni tive, given the way Maxine snored, but it was the principle of the thing. At the breakfast table, he had read the back of the raisin bran box because she had grabbed the paper first. All for a night at the fights with August? Forget it.

"You're looking good, Larry," August said.

"You look awful."

"No, I mean it."

"We got home earlier than usual. We got home. I got a good night's sleep."

August squeezed his arm and nodded, his face screwed up in an odd way. Gridiron sniffed discreetly. August probably had a snootful already. Wilma Trout claimed he plied her with drink every time he lured her into his office.

"He's got to drink, Wilma."

"Got to?"

"It's kind of embarrassing to explain."

She had crowded close. "Tell me."

43

"August has an almost uncontrollable sex drive. Still. Alcohol is the only thing that enables him to keep control of himself."

Wilma backed away, a wondering expression on her weasel face. The mystery of the male gender. Was there no end to it?

Larry said to August now, "I have to get home."

"Of course. I don't mean to delay you."

If August was sober he was slightly nuts, but then, by this time in the afternoon no one was exactly *compos mentis*. Nonetheless, Gridiron did not like the way August kept looking at him as they walked down the corridor.

"You told Bledsoe yet, August?"

That snapped August out of it. "Tell him? Don't be crazy."

"When the poem comes out, he'll know he didn't write it."

After a moment, August said, "Don't be so sure. Even so, he doesn't have to tell anybody. Meanwhile, he can follow up with more poems, as many as he can afford."

"Afford?"

August explained as they stood on the steps outside in the balmy September air. Imagine, paying to get published. Vanity of vanities. Poor Bledsoe. Maybe August was right. What difference did it make that he paid to get printed? His money would be better spent on Henry VIII than on his own stuff anyway. Even so, Gridiron didn't like it. This escapade revealed a side of August he did not like. Joking was one thing, but you had to draw the line somewhere. An idea came over the horizon of Gridiron's mind and caused him to smile. August was looking at him strangely again.

"See you tomorrow, August."

"Absolutely!"

August had to be drunk. The thought of having a beer when he got home added to the euphoria Gridiron felt at the thought that he was going to tell Bledsoe what August Frye had done to him.

"Why?" Maxine asked. They had made up and were having somewhat unseasonal gin and tonics.

"It's not right what he did to Bledsoe."

"Since when did you become such a boy scout?" Maxine did freelance copyediting, having preferred to continue working while the kids were growing up. It was a job where there was low tolerance of BS.

"Okay. Just say I want to play a little trick on August."

"Your old friend."

"Don't be so sure."

"You go out together once a week and make fools of yourselves. If that isn't friendship, what is?"

It would have sounded petty to mention the things Bledsoe had passed on to him. The younger man disliked tattling, but Gridiron got the picture. The trouble was, it was so easy to believe. August Frye currying favor with the young by running down his ostensible friends. And just for the hell of it. August really did not want whatever advancement could come his way at Lyndon Johnson. He was perfectly content to meet his illiterate classes and hope that some sliver of light might reach into the recesses of one of those disadvantaged minds. But to be head of the department, to be given a teaching award—these he would regard as defeats rather than victories. And Gridiron agreed with him all the way.

"I had an interesting phone call today," Maxine said, plucking the slice of lime from her glass and sucking on it.

Gridiron waited. Maxine's playful tone was uncharacteristic.

"From her majesty the dean."

"Maggie?"

"How many deans are there?"

"What is she calling you for?"

"Now don't get all excited. Listen. She wanted to enlist my help in persuading you to become the new chair of the department."

"Oh no, she doesn't. Not on your life."

"Why not! You make a good chair, we could use the extra money, it's an honor, of course you want it."

"Did you tell her that?"

Maxine considered her answer before giving it. "Let's just say I promised to do all I could."

Maxine lifted her glass and smiled sweetly. Forty years of marriage gave her some rights, maybe, but this was too much. However happy it might make her, all he could think of was the reaction of his colleagues. All right, of August Frye. The son of a bitch wouldn't let on, of course. He would congratulate Larry and promise him all the cooperation in the world, his manner would be impeccable, he would never let on. But inside he would be doubled over with laughter, and Larry Gridiron would know it. Worse, August would himself have turned down the job. August was Maggie's first choice. Having spurned the promotion himself would give him moral authority over anyone who should have said no and didn't.

Larry didn't argue with Maxine. For one thing, he would have lost and he couldn't face the prospect of another night on the couch, snoring or no snoring. Somehow he would escape being appointed chair. If it came to that, he would lie to Maggie. He could tell her, confidentially of course, that he was seriously ill, and beg her not to tell Maxine. Obviously, he could not be asked to take on the responsibility of chair. Not in his condition. He smiled. It was a ploy worthy of August himself.

August. He would now most definitely speak to Bledsoe about that poem. Two can play the moral-authority game.

12

BLEDSOE WANTED TO CRY out when August Frye got up
and left him alone with Hastings. Hastings had been in
Bledsoe's class the year before and failed it miserably. The
poor fellow was illiterate. He could not read the assignments
with comprehension, his discussions of them were something out of Evelyn Waugh at his racist worst, yet he seemed
to think that it was simply a matter of Bledsoe's opinion
against his. And his present manner now struck the poet
professor as menacing.

"I gotta pass this course."

"But you *don't* got to, Roy. You don't even have to take it."

"I want to take it. Last year you failed me. This year I'm
gonna pass."

Bledsoe did not want to ask Hastings to sit down. On the
other hand, it was distinctly unnerving to have him looming
over his desk, staring down unblinkingly.

"How'd I do in the first quiz?"

The blue books were in the drawer of Bledsoe's desk. He
had not corrected them yet, but he had looked at Hastings's.
It was top of the pile, the last one turned in, the poor devil
sitting like Gulliver in a too-small seat frowning at his blue
book long after the others were gone. He had managed to
write half a page of something remotely resembling English

prose. He was supposed to have written on four essay
questions, questions that had intentionally given scope to
the students, permitting them to range freely so that Bledsoe
could find out if there were any good ones among them.
Themes such as Dickens's Social Conscience invited the
student to expatiate on the power of fiction to effect social
change. There were seven possibilities in all, so there was
room for choice before the student even began. Bledsoe did
not look forward to the crushing disappointment he knew
reading those blue books would be. But the worst remaining
blue book would be light-years better than the inarticulate
effort of Roy Hastings.

"I haven't corrected them yet."

"I passed."

"Which questions did you treat?"

"I passed," Hastings repeated, glaring at Bledsoe.

"Of course you passed," the poet squeaked.

Hastings showed no elation at having effected this be-
trayal of the minimal standards of Western civilization. He
nodded, turned, and left. Bledsoe realized he was drenched
with sweat. He got up and locked the door, returned to his
desk, and sat shivering with fear and self-loathing. He found
a bottle of brandy in August's desk and poured himself half
a Styrofoam cup full and tossed it off.

He did not consider what he had done cowardly. Imagine
telling that monster he would flunk the course again. It
would be foolhardy to arouse Hastings. Courage had nothing
to do with it. He poured out some more brandy, emptying
the bottle. He must remember to replace it.

After finishing the brandy, he turned off the lights and sat
on in the office. When finally he left, it was with the real fear
that Roy Hastings was lurking somewhere in the dark,
intent on driving home the point that he was gonna pass
that course this year.

Bledsoe wrote poetry until two in the morning, on his
computer, but nothing seemed as good as "Fronds." What
if he had only one poem accepted, nothing more, just the

one? It would seem a freak. It would be a freak. He had to get more acceptances as soon as he could so there would be no doubt that he was indeed at last a recognized poet.

Perhaps it was wrong to rhyme, but it was the one thing he could not willingly eradicate from his efforts. Frye had liked his device of rhyming words other than those ending a line. Tonight he experimented with front rhyme.

> Ending our relationship is like
> Sending spaceship earth out of the
> Galaxy. Do not write or wire,
> Telex me that our relationship obtains.

Bledsoe stared at these lines, wanting to like them but unable to. He needed music in his lines, a lilt and lift. Tomorrow he would follow Auden's lead and others, write new lyrics to old songs, write to the rhythm of nursery rhymes.

He woke to the sound of the telephone. It was a telegram. His head was foggy, and excitement over receiving a wire garbled the message. It was from the editor of the *Nor'easter*, but what was the operator saying?

"You want it sent out to you?"

"Yes. Yes, I have to read it."

He gave the address of his campus office and set off unshaven for Lyndon Johnson, a bumpy ride on the express bus, through the Bronx, past the Park, down to Twenty-third, fretting all the way. He should have had the wire read again, written it down, then asked them to send it. It took a real effort not to admit he had heard a certain word in that message, a word that had rendered him numb.

He put on Mr. Coffee and settled down to wait. He skipped his class, not wanting to be elsewhere when the wire came. August Frye was surprised to find him at his desk when he should have been lecturing.

"I'm expecting an important letter."

August let it go, thank God. Two hours went by. Stanley went down the hall to a public phone and called Western

Union, wondering when he could expect a copy of the wire. He was put on hold for an aging three minutes.

"That already went out, sir."

"Thank you."

He drank five cups of strong coffee, and still the wire did not arrive. When he tried again to reach Western Union, the line was busy. Haddock was with August when Blesdoe returned to the office.

"This came to the dean's office by mistake, Stanley. It was opened by mistake. Sorry."

Stanley took the wire and sat at his desk, turning away from Frye and Haddock, who in any case ignored him. He opened the wire furtively, feeling like a gambler in a Western movie, revealing the smallest sliver of the card to see what it was. But then he opened the wire wide.

> Disregard letter accepting "Fronds." Your attempted plagiarism caught in time. Submit nothing further here.
>
> Hector Ackrill

He left the wire on his desk. He did not say anything to Frye or Haddock.

It would be three days before he would be seen again.

August Frye identified the body.

PART TWO

▽

The Name of Action

$\triangledown$

1

AUGUST MUST HAVE NOTICED Stanley leave the office, but in all truth he had been surprised that his office mate was not there when the delegation from his class turned up to find out where their professor was.

Haddock had been in the midst of an elaborate joke about a one-legged passenger and a blond stewardess, and was not interrupted easily. He continued to tell the story on their way to the classroom. August opened the door and looked at what he suspected was all too fair a sample of Stanley Bledsoe's class in The Novel as News. Stanley pretty well ignored plot and character as he went in pursuit of hints as to dress, money, class awareness, etc., in nineteenth-century novels on both sides of the water. August had heard him *usque ad nauseam* on tobacco and spitting in mid-nine-teenth-century America, but then, that had been Stanley's dissertation topic at NYU. "Great Expectorations and Nine-teenth-Century British Novelists."

"He won't be meeting his class today," August said, telling them what they already knew.

"What do you mean you're out of tissue?" Haddock shouted behind him. It was the punch line of his joke.

"We know he isn't here," said a small female with steel-wool hair, steel-rimmed glasses, and a steely look to match.

53

"He was going to return our exams today."

"I seen him here earlier." This was said by the massive linebacker-sized student who had visited Stanley the day before.

"I know. He's been called away." In his eagerness to get rid of them and have Haddock explain his joke, August made a grievous error. "I suggest you telephone Professor Bledsoe this afternoon."

All afternoon the telephone on Stanley's desk rang angrily, the more so when August stopped answering it. His message was not well received. They didn't care where Bledsoe was; they wanted to know what grade they'd received on last week's quiz.

"He this Bledsoe listed in the Bronx?" a surly student asked.

"I don't know," August said. "The directory must be full of Bledsoes."

The university operator had no way to stop calls coming in. August sought refuge in the lounge, where a sibilant exchange among Weinstein, Stella, and Quinlan had been going on.

"Gridiron's with the dean." Aaron Weinstein searched Frye's face when he said this.

It was late in the day for the coffee in the lounge to be still potable, but August loaded it up with fake sugar and cream and took a chance.

"Has Stanley been in here?"

None of his colleagues spoke. They seemed to be weighing the remark for political significance, relevance to his or her own career, and with general suspicion.

"He came in this morning but didn't meet his class. He must have stepped out when I wasn't looking."

Stella said, "Did you check the men's room?"

"Why, is he there?"

Despite himself, Aaron smiled, revealing irregular teeth. Quinlan didn't get it.

"It's your turf, not mine," Stella said, proving again that

wit and a trembling lip are strangers to one another.

The annoyance of the phone calls made August angry at Stanley rather than concerned. Bledsoe would not be the first professor who had granted himself a one-day leave of absence and gone off to watch six hours of movies, get drunk, do research in the public library, or simply get bloated on junk food, blotting the life of the mind from the mind. Playing hooky.

But that night when he left, August turned off the Mr. Coffee. It was as full as it had been that morning after Stanley made a second pot.

The next day was Friday. August answered Stanley's phone, half expecting it to be the missing poet professor. But it was only irate students. One voice became familiar.

"What's your name?"

"You gonna give me my grade?"

"How many times have you called?"

"I want my grade."

"Give me your name, please."

"Roy Hastings."

August put down the phone. Hastings had been slamming the phone down on him regularly, and it seemed only right that he be repaid in kind. No one answered the phone at Stanley's apartment in the Bronx. Strange. He lived with his father, or at least he had. August realized how little he knew of Bledsoe, despite their year's cohabitation. The urban college is not a community, particularly if it is called a community college. Strangers emerge from buses and subways and fulfill daytime roles and then disappear once more, going back whence they have come. That he and Larry Gridiron and a few of the older hands knew one another was due to longevity and the fact that they had secured apartments relatively close by that rent control enabled them to keep. God only knew where the new ones lived. Queens, Staten Island, Brooklyn. There was a mathematician who came from Philadelphia three times a week. They should offer their courses on television and get it over with.

August showed Larry Gridiron the telegram. Neither of them touched it. They read it standing behind Stanley's chair.

"The poor sonofabitch," Larry said.

"Plagiarism is a little strong."

"Well, misdirected. What are you going to do, August?"

"What do you mean?"

"You have to get him off the hook. You sent the poem in, he didn't."

August's angry reaction was an index of the rightness of Larry's accusation. He did not admit this, of course. Damage control, as the politicians say, would be easy. No one knew about the poem except the editor and presumably some of his staff, Stanley, and themselves. August drafted a letter for Stanley after Larry had left.

Dear Hector,

Thank you for your wire drawing attention to my office mate's practical joke. As you noticed, he slipped an updated version of a lyric of Henry VIII's into the poems I sent for your consideration. Perhaps I need not explain academic humor to you. Of course, I understand your indignation. Imagine mine. I hope you will find my other poems suitable for appearance in the *Nor'easter*.

Fondly,

Just the thing, August decided, looking it over. Only a churl would refuse this explanation. And after all, Hector occupied no moral eminence, exploiting poor devils like Stanley who longed to see their work in print. Larry read it over and nodded.

"Good."

"Now, if I can find Stanley."

"Call his home."

"No one answers."

"He's got a father, doesn't he?"

"That's right." He felt he owed it to Stanley to sound sure.

August tried to think that Stanley's disappearance had nothing to do with the poem and the telegram. He was just playing hooky. Disappearance was too strong a word. The fact that August hadn't seen him didn't mean Stanley had disappeared.

Saturday morning, he spent an hour trying to get an answer from the phone in the Bronx. Just before noon, he decided to pay Stanley a visit at home. He had with him the draft of the letter to the editor of the *Nor'easter*. Five minutes with Stanley and this whole thing could be cleared up.

For years August had survived New York by imagining he had just arrived, would soon be on his way to somewhere habitable and in the meanwhile could enjoy the natives. This became more and more difficult to do as the years went by. It was impossible in the claustrophobic intimacy of the subway. But he made it to the Bronx and tried to imagine it was fresh air he was breathing as he went up the street to Stanley's building.

The typed legend "Bledsoe, F & S" was scotch-taped to one of the mailboxes in the hall, unpolished bronze, a communication system—press button, speak into grill—that did not inspire confidence. He could get no response. He went downstairs to the basement and knocked on the superintendent's door. From the other side came the roar of rock music. A student?

August caught the attention of the occupant during a change of records. Ponytail, mustache, earrings, black T-shirt, jeans, and bare feet. He looked insolently out at August Frye.

"I'm trying to get in touch with the Bledsoes. On four."

"Yeah?"

"It's important."

"You a bill collector?"

The impulse to give a withering reply, drawing attention to his position at Lyndon Johnson Community College and the whole vague aura of prestige supposedly consequent on that, was strong. But August could see that this wretch would be more aggrieved than impressed by claims to eminence.

"I work with Stanley."

"The professor?"

"That's right."

"You a professor?" Skeptical eyes took his measure and seemed to find him wanting.

"Yes. It's very important that I talk to Stanley."

"Did you try telephoning?"

"No one answers."

"They're up there. I saw the old man this morning."

"Could I go up, please? They don't answer the call bell."

"It doesn't work."

"Well, that explains that." Careful, careful, he was doing just fine and he didn't want to ruin it with sarcasm.

The young man slipped on sandals and led him upstairs to the fourth floor. He banged mercilessly on the door for half a minute. His grin revealed a missing tooth.

"Deaf," he explained.

He raised his fist to punish the panel again, but there was the sound of locks unlocking and the rustle of chains. The door opened a crack, and one rheumy eye looked out at them.

"Mr. Bledsoe? I'm August Frye. I have to talk with Stanley."

"You gotta yell. Loud."

August repeated it, louder. The super pushed him aside, put his face into the opening, and yelled, "Open the goddam door. It's okay. It's Norman." He stepped back so the old man could enjoy the reassuring sight of him. The door closed, the chain was removed, and the door opened again.

"Thank you," August said to the super.

The young man nodded, smiling his Halloween smile, and held out his hand. August gave him a dollar. It was more than worth it. The superintendent shared this view. His hand remained out. Five dollars was required to send him on his way. The old man—baggy pants, blue work shirt, slippers—followed this with interest. He stepped back, and August went in.

The living room was small and crowded with furniture.

August had a glimpse of a narrow hallway that went between closed doors to the open door of a bathroom.

"I would like to speak with Stanley. My name is August Frye."

The old man's mouth opened and he watched August carefully, but no comprehension showed on his face. August stopped.

"Stanley," he shouted.

The old man nodded.

"August Frye." Pointing at himself. "Friend Stanley."

White man speaks to noble savage. If he had enough colored beads, he could buy the Bronx. But he was getting through. The old man pushed away from the arm of the sofa against which he had been leaning. He drew attention to an item on the wall. August recognized it. Stanley's degree from NYU. Magna cum loudmouth, as the Kingfish would say. Stanley had tried to hang it on the office wall, but there wasn't enough room. For a few weeks, he had propped it against the bookcases, then given up and taken it home.

"Where is Stanley?"

"Where is Stanley?"

The old man was not repeating his question, but asking his own. August stayed for half an hour more, trying to have a conversation with the old man. It was impossible. The huge plastic bugs in each of Mr. Bledsoe's ears seemed to prevent rather than aid hearing. Had Hitler targeted the hard of hearing too? When he left, he did not think the old man knew who he was or why exactly he had come. But Mr. Bledsoe seemed content. Perhaps he took the visit as indicating all was fine with Stanley.

The stairway seemed narrower than when he had mounted it behind the super. He was aware of muffled sounds, as if the walls were occupied. It was a relief to get outside again. He felt that in any case he had attempted to do a good work. Even Larry Gridiron should approve.

And then he saw Stanley.

He was seated in a car parked at the curb, big as life,

staring straight ahead in the preoccupied manner that was familiar to August Frye. He went down to the car and tapped on the window. No response. Experience with Bledsoe senior had made Frye resourceful. He took out his keys and tapped on the window with those. Stanley stared resolutely ahead. August tried the door, but it was locked. He tapped on the window again.

Passersby were noticing that he was being ignored. Angry, he banged on the window with his whole bunch of keys. Stanley did not even blink. August stooped to get a better look. Minutes went by, and Stanley did not blink. He did not seem to be breathing, either. It occurred to August that Stanley was dead.

He turned and went inside the building.

$\triangledown$

2

"GUY NAMED AUGUST FRYE wants to talk to you."

If someone had rolled a Molotov cocktail into the precinct, Cable would have been less startled. It was like turning on TV and seeing JFK, still president, still forty-three years old, nothing changed.

"Is he here?"

Marla, who had enough body for two and not because she was pregnant, never looked at the one to whom she spoke. She told the wall that Frye was on the phone. Cable snatched it up.

"Sergeant Cable."

"James, this is Professor Frye. August Frye." Cable would have recognized that mellifluent voice without help. "Have you read about my unfortunate colleague, Stanley Bledsoe?"

Cable smiled and closed his eyes. Why should the reminder of failure make him feel so good? Frye had directed his misbegotten thesis, or tried to. The finished product had been turned down by the committee when Frye sent it on with a neutral accompanying letter. He did not want to make the negative judgment alone. Perhaps he was wrong. He was right. So James B. Cable ended up a master manqué. Frye's phrase. He suggested that Cable adopt the initials ABD—all but dissertation—used by candidates for the Ph.D. who had completed course requirements, passed their written and oral candidacy examinations, and had only to complete their dissertations. But when Cable walked away from Lyndon Johnson, he had wiped the dust of the place from his shoes in the recommended manner. He had never been back. And now this call from August Frye.

"Bledsoe? I don't know him."

"He came after your time, James. A young man. He's dead."

Cable waited. So did Frye. What did he expect him to say? That he was sorry?

"It happened in the Bronx. Actually, I feel quite badly about it. Look, could we get together?"

"What made you call me after all these years?"

"How many former students do I have on the police force?"

"That's kind of a zinger."

"I meant it as praise."

Cable arranged to call on August Frye at his office. Fifteen years on the NYPD had put fiber in his soul, but James Cable felt a lump in his throat as he scuffed through the fallen leaves on the walkways of Lyndon Johnson Community College. Filthy place, bums on the benches, wire trash receptacles the target of bag people, a vendor selling frankfurters and hot pretzels, where were the students? But Cable was stepping into the past, and he saw these buildings as they had been when new, monuments to the Great Society, every man a Ph.D., to hell with Harvard and the Ivy League. It was a James Cable with fifteen years shaved off and animated with hope who went up the steps and inside and took the battered elevator to the second floor. There was a directory. English Department. Chair: George Blair. A list of names, most of them unfamiliar, but some almost as evocative as August Frye's. L. Gridiron. S. Houston. W. Trout. Wilma, ye gods. He stooped over a water fountain to gather his emotions, and then went down the hall and knocked on Frye's door.

Frye looked older, of course, but was unmistakably the same man Cable had admired and hated years before. They shook hands, stood looking at one another across Frye's desk for half a minute, and then Frye laughed.

"I couldn't have picked you out of a lineup. Is that the term?"

"My hair is thinner."

"Who wants fat hair?"

Cable looked around the office. "I don't remember this place."

"I've only been in it two years. I shared it with a young colleague named Stanley Bledsoe. He died the week before last. That's why I called you."

Cable had checked out Bledsoe before coming. Stanley Bledsoe, aged 33, had been found dead in a locked automobile parked in the street outside his residence in the Bronx. Cause of death? Asphyxiation. The deceased had also suffered what could have been a mortal blow to the forehead. But there were no signs of violence, nothing in the car or on the person of the deceased to suggest foul play. The car in which the body had been found did not belong to Bledsoe. It had been reported stolen by the owner two days before Bledsoe's body was found. Odd circumstances, no doubt of that, but there were always odd circumstances when you looked into anything at all closely. Cable was not surprised that no further action was being taken at this time.

"I feel responsible for his death," Frye said.

Cable accepted a cup of coffee and got comfortable. This was why Frye had telephoned him.

It seemed that Frye had gotten along well enough with Bledsoe but basically thought the young man was ridiculous. His ambition to be a poet was a case in point, but there were as well his obsessive publishing, the fuss he made over the teaching award, the agitation to get promoted. It sounded normal enough to Cable.

Sending in an altered lyric of Henry VIII to a magazine using Bledsoe's name struck Cable as mean rather than funny. He could easily understand why Bledsoe would take the charge of plagiarism as hard as he did.

"But that could have been fixed up in a minute."

Cable looked doubtful, and Frye showed him the draft of a letter.

"When did Bledsoe write this?"

"He didn't. I did. I felt I owed him that. This is why I was so anxious to find him, to get him to send off this letter and clear the air."

Cable wondered if Bledsoe would have been anxious to have Frye write more things for him, after the poem. There was no doubt about it, August Frye had not covered himself with honor in this episode.

"What did he say when you told him?"

August Frye looked at him blankly.

"Did you tell him you had sent the poem?"

"I would have. When I showed him this letter." Frye spoke as if he were trying to persuade himself. Cable was looking at a man who understandably felt guilt. The question was, what did he expect James B. Cable to do about it?

"I'm sure he was killed, James."

"What makes you think so?"

"It's the only thing that makes sense."

"If there was need to explain his death, suicide would be a far more likely explanation if the circumstances did not tell against it. His career was blighted, he had been made an ass out of by colleagues he thought liked and admired him, he would shortly become both a laughingstock and an object of censure. Plagiarism is still a serious charge, isn't it?"

August Frye visibly winced each time Cable added a new element to the weight that had been pressing down on Bledsoe. No wonder Frye felt guilty. His guilt would diminish considerably if someone could be found who had killed Bledsoe. But that service the NYPD was not going to be able to provide Professor August Frye.

"The car was full of exhaust fumes. He didn't just stop breathing in a stolen automobile, James."

"That's what the preliminary coroner's report says."

"Preliminary?"

"You don't want to know how long it takes to get the definitive report."

"Then it's possible it will be seen as due to unnatural causes?"

"Only if by possible you mean it wouldn't violate the principle of contradiction."

"His students hated him, James."

"Yes?"

Frye seemed to be wrestling with his conscience. He won. "James, one of those students, a huge illiterate fellow, threatened Stanley several times in my hearing. Stanley lived in terror of him. The fellow flunked the course last year but signed up for it again. The same course. He called here asking for Stanley while he was missing. He knew Stanley lived in the Bronx."

It was a proof of Frye's emotional involvement that he thought what he said added up to a coherent understanding of what had happened to Stanley Bledsoe.

"Professor Frye, if there was foul play in Bledsoe's death, and nothing we know suggests there was, I would bet that neither his literary ambitions nor his students had anything to do with it. How well did you know Stanley Bledsoe, apart from what you learned here at LBJCC?"

Almost nothing. The trip to the Bronx had been August's first. The members of the English Department did not socialize, for reasons too complicated for August to go into.

"Something may turn up to get the people in the Bronx interested in this, but don't count on it."

"The autopsy."

"Particularly don't expect any revelation from that."

"Isn't there anything you can do?"

"No."

"I'm disappointed."

"I can't lie to you. I can see why you feel badly about Bledsoe's death, but . . . "

"Roy Hastings," Frye said in low, urgent tones. "He is the student I mentioned before. Can't you find out what he was doing during the days Stanley was missing?"

James took down the address of the student, but he did not make any promises. Frye offered him another cup of coffee. He would have taken it if he thought the conversation could get off the subject of Bledsoe. But Frye's present disposition was obviously against that's happening.

"It's good just talking about this with someone else," Frye said.

"I understand."

"I keep thinking of Stanley's father. He's deaf as a post, the poor man. What will become of him?"

They parted with earnest statements that they must get together very soon just to talk about the past. But James, somewhat to his own surprise, was glad to pull Frye's door shut after him.

During the next two weeks, as opportunity afforded, he kept an eye on what the precinct in the Bronx was doing about Stanley Bledsoe. It wasn't much.

$\triangledown$

3

ONE BRISK OCTOBER MORNING Gridiron saw the story over
the shoulder of a man ahead of him on the bus, but read
only the opening paragraph before the man turned the page.
He tapped the man's shoulder.

"Could I see the page you just turned?"

The man ignored him. A young woman beside Gridiron
went rigid, staring straight ahead. Any unusual behavior on
a bus put passengers on guard. Aha. The girl had a *Daily
News* clutched in her hand.

"Miss, could I look at your paper?"

She stiffened more and stared straight ahead.

"I'll buy it from you."

Her eyes widened. For God's sake. He reached for the
paper. The woman screamed. She stood and kept on scream-
ing. This turned out to Gridiron's advantage. He got out of
his seat, and the woman fled past him. Gridiron looked
around at no one in particular, shrugged, and sat down.
What was the world coming to?

He had to see that paper. Bledsoe. LBJ. Already he had a
sinking feeling that this went back to Cable.

It had been perhaps a week or two after Bledsoe's funeral,
if you could call it that. One afternoon Gridiron came out
of his office and as he was shutting the door heard Frye's

open and close. Sometimes he felt August was lying in wait
for him, so synchronized were their arrivals and departures
now. But he turned to see James B. Cable standing there.

It wasn't only relief at not having to deal with Frye that
made him happy to see the Once and Future Student, as
Cable had been known during his prolonged stay among
them. Gridiron led him down the hall before asking what he
was doing on campus, but the fact that he had been visiting
Frye seemed an omen.

"Were you coming to see me?"

"I'm checking with all members of my examining board.
There's some thought I should reactivate my candidacy."

In the seconds before he saw Cable was joking, Gridiron
knew a great depression. Cable was not stupid; he had
certain gifts. But he had no feel for literature, he was lost in
the great critics and commentators, and such teaching as he
had done as an assistant had been disastrous. Cable was one
of those people determined to do the one thing God had not
meant him to do. The try had to end either in tragedy or
farce. Cable managed a bit of both. Pity to fail the oral as he
had done, but he had enlivened their lives with his answers.

"What is the earliest extant work in the English vernacular?"

"Extant?"

"Yes."

"As in formerly?"

It emerged that Cable thought "tant" was an adjective
and "ex" a prefix. That he also thought Chaucer's clerk had
worked in an Oxford store, that Piers Plowman was a hired
hand of someone named Pierce, and that the dark lady of
the sonnets was the daughter of Desdemona and Othello
added spice to the afternoon. Gridiron's favorite was Cable's
gloss on the significance of the phrase "the sun also rises"
as an Easter motif. They all had learned much that day. It
was good to see this confident, successful, worldly Cable,
willing to laugh off past disappointments. Frye had called
Cable about Bledsoe.

"We can get a drink across the street."

"Just a beer," Cable said.

Gridiron put Cable on the one available stool and stood next to him with his beer.

"What did he tell you?"

"Frye thinks someone killed Bledsoe."

"He thinks he did."

"He sure feels bad about it."

"He should. Did he tell you why he feels bad? Of course he did. It's like going to confession. Load it onto everybody else. Only, it doesn't work for him. He still feels guilty."

"Do you know a student named Hastings?"

"Jesus!"

"No, Roy." A little delay before Cable punched his arm. Gridiron punched him back.

"He told you Hastings killed Bledsoe because he flunked his course, right? Well, Hastings flunked the course, but that is the extent of it."

They had three beers before parting, but Gridiron wasn't sure he was having any effect. It turned out the police weren't really pursuing the matter anyway. So both he and Frye had wasted their time.

"August tell you about the department?"

Cable shrugged, and Gridiron searched his face for duplicity. Was it possible that August had passed up an opportunity to tell their failed student that Larry Gridiron was now chair of the department? What a tale of declension August could make of that. But perhaps he kept his mordant remarks for faculty and active students. Larry had a fourth beer by himself, pondering the disfavor to which he had come.

And now this story in the *Daily News*!

There was a message from the dean when he got to the departmental office, but when he called Maggie Downs, Haddock said she was with Hackis.

"About the *Daily News*?"

"Yup."

"Tell her I called."

He closed himself in. One thing about being chair, he had a private office. Chair. Why the hell had he accepted the job? Maxine, that's why, though what advantage it had for her he didn't know. My husband the chairman? Probably that was all she wanted. Maggie's reaction when he told her he was too ill to accept the job had been strange.

"Lyndon Johnson does not discriminate on the basis of race, creed, sex, age, or health."

"Or intelligence?"

A mistake. A mortally ill man does not fool around. Kid around. It was Maggie and Hackis who fooled around, if the stories were true. He told Maxine they picked him because they wanted a swinger. Frye was so shaken by Bledsoe's death that he actually seemed to mean it when he congratulated Gridiron on his appointment.

"I did everything to get out of it, August. I even told her I was too sick for the job."

August squeezed his arm, and there seemed to be tears in his eyes. Had Maggie chosen Larry in order to make his obituary more impressive? City College Chair Collapses.

"You wearing contacts?"

"What are they, deodorant pads?"

Old friends again, that seemed to be it. So Gridiron became chair, Frye brooded over the death of his office mate to the extent of calling in Cable, and today they had a story in the *Daily News* they didn't need.

He picked up the phone and dialed August's number. Busy.

4

GREGORY HACKIS HAD INSTALLED tinted windows in the presidential car so that during his daily shuttling between his apartment on Sixty-third Street and his presidential office at LBJ he was not the target of curious eyes. Having a chauffeur was an ambiguous thing in a democracy.

Priscilla, his driver, wore her cap low over her eyes and seemed intent on keeping things egalitarian behind the tinted glass.

"Will you look at the son of a bitch?" she demanded, and leaned on the horn.

Hackis did not look. He had his briefcase open, he had a folder open, he was shuffling paper, ostensibly busy. Busy not getting into a conversation with Priscilla.

"See the *Daily News*?"

He murmured that he had not, keeping his head down.

"Here." She tossed it over the seat, and it knocked his manila folder to the floor. "Page three or five, in around there."

"What is it?"

"About our dead professor."

"Our what!"

"Bledsoe. It looks like they're investigating it."

Hackis picked up the folder and its contents, shoved them

71

into his attaché case, and began to page through the tabloid.
Murder? Investigation? Bledsoe?

"PD Probes Poet Prof's Strange Death." The story was like
a telegram to the illiterate, a type of prose in which Hackis
himself had become adept as president of LBJ. There was a
flattering photograph of the campus, just buildings and
grounds, not a student or derelict in sight. A picture of
Bledsoe. Had he really looked that young? A picture of the
street in the Bronx where the body was found "under
mysterious circumstances." Anonymous sources in the police and on the faculty were cited, but there was only one
who was named. Lawrence Gridiron.

Hackis picked up his phone and called his office.

"Francis, I want to see Professor Gridiron this morning,
as soon as possible.

"The *Daily News*?"

"Yes. And Farkas. I want to see Farkas, too."

"Gridiron. Farkas." He could picture Francis nodding as
he jotted them down. "Downs?"

"Good idea. Did we have any idea this was in the works?"

"No, we didn't. I cannot speak for Farkas, of course. He
should have known. And Gridiron knew, of course."

Priscilla seemed to be enjoying having upset him, but the
traffic soon captured her profane attention.

In the back seat, closed attaché case on his lap, hands flat
on its top, President Hackis considered how to control the
impact of that story. That the story did nothing but sensa-
tionalize the facts of Bledsoe's death was neither here nor
there. Now the story was the story. Politics had prepared
Hackis well for his current post. It was simply another
political task, as far as he could see, and the name of the
task this morning was damage control.

"This will simplify the new chair's problems," Maggie had
said at the memorial services for Blair. "We'd already decided
to cut back English by three. With Blair gone, all the new
chair has to do is get rid of two."

And now Bledsoe was gone. Hadn't Stanley himself said

something about the attrition rate in the English Department? The thought that he'd had a premonition consoled him somewhat. He would refer to it when he saw Maggie.

Maggie. Only Priscilla knew for sure, and he thought he could count on her discretion.

"You want to know what I think?" Priscilla had said the second time she dropped him off at Maggie's.

"No."

"She's one ambitious broad. She'll squeeze you like an orange and throw you away. George Sanders."

"George who?"

"One of Zsa Zsa Gabor's husbands."

"Nice image."

He meant it. He liked the thought that Maggie was squeezing him. As for the throwing away, they would see about that. But Priscilla as conscience was a pain in the ass. He wished he had discouraged her egalitarian tendency to think of them as a team. Of course Priscilla felt protective about Joyce, although she refused to drive Joyce anywhere. Joyce wasn't president, and Priscilla said presidents' wives didn't count. He should have fought her on that. She had to drive Maggie when he told her to, Maggie was in administration and, who knew, it could be in the line of duty, even though Priscilla knew better. Apart from lecturing him over her shoulder, her only alternative was to create a scandal and jeopardize her job. And then Maggie learned that Priscilla was shacking up with a student, and that had put him back in the driver's seat, more or less.

The *Daily News* was clearly trying to create a scandal over poor Bledsoe. Did it jeopardize Gregory Hackis's job? He ran a nervous hand over his wavy red hair, narrowed his eyes, and looked at the world through the pink thicket of his lashes. His jaw was bony, his nose short, his chest broad. His cross was that he stood only five foot eight. The presidency of LBJ—he always identified himself with a little chuckle, lest anyone think he himself was impressed—was a stepping-stone, one more rung on the ladder he had taken

from Lincoln, Nebraska, to Washington, to HEW, and on to
LBJ. Where next? Half the fun of his affair with Maggie was
that, sated and sipping diet drinks, they could lie beneath
her sheets and talk career. Maggie wanted his job. He must
go on to greater things.

A dark thought crossed his mind as they inched past the
Plaza. If the Bledsoe thing could jeopardize his job, then the
Bledsoe story was in Maggie's interest.

He picked up his phone again.

"Francis? I want to see Dean Downs first."

In the rearview mirror, Priscilla's eyes looked at him with
disappointment.

5

"**W**HAT DO YOU know about this story in the *Daily News*?" August asked when he got through to Cable.

"I was going to ask you the same thing."

"There's nothing to it?"

"What did it tell you that you don't already know?"

"But who told the paper?"

A pause. "Something has happened."

The owner of the stolen car in which Bledsoe's body was found was Priscilla Cortez.

"So?"

"She drives for Gregory Hackis."

Priscilla's car was stolen, she told police, not from the area of LBJ but in Brooklyn where she lived. During the week, she drove the college limo back and forth to work and did not need to use her own car. Cable was not done, however.

"She has been going out with a student. A man named Hastings."

There were relatively fresh fingerprints in the car they had been unable to match. Hastings?

"I wonder if there are any here in the office," Frye said, but Cable could not get an authorization for such a speculative expenditure.

"I had hoped you could get a set for me, Professor Frye."

"I'll do it," he cried.

After hanging up, Frye took out his bottle of brandy for the first time since Bledsoe had disappeared. The bottle was empty. No matter, he toasted the empty chair with coffee from Bledsoe's machine. August felt he could take some credit at least for the new turn in the investigation of Bledsoe's death. Cable had been named liaison with the precinct in the Bronx, having drawn attention to his knowledge of LBJ.

August Frye had taken the precaution of locking his door because of the *Daily News* story, and he neither answered the phone nor responded to knocking. He sat silently now while Gridiron put a tattoo on the door.

"August, you in there? It's Larry."

The chairman's tone suggested his embarrassment at standing in the hallway addressing a closed door.

"I know you're in there, August. I'm getting the janitor with a key."

Bluffing, of course. Frye wanted solitude, he wanted to be alone here where the ghost of Bledsoe could be of assistance. What had happened to his young friend during the three days that intervened between his leaving this office and being found dead in a car outside his Bronx home?

Bledsoe's courses had been canceled, to some grumbling from students. The fact that they had already taken an exam in the class was mentioned. The exams! Surely Hastings's fingerprints would be on the blue book he had turned in.

Bledsoe's desk was locked, but of course August Frye knew that his office mate hid the key beneath a copy of *Jane Eyre* ("Jane Eyre?" "Mrs. Rochester." Ah. The mad wife locked in the attic. "That's pretty obvious, Stanley.")

It was odd to think that the key he took from beneath the Brontë novel had been put there by the then living hand of Stanley Bledsoe. Somber thought. But this office was the occasion of many somber thoughts.

The examinations were not in the desk. He looked in every drawer, twice, but found no stack of blue books. Sitting in

Stanley's chair, pudgy and perplexed, August Frye considered the possibilities. Stanley might have taken the examinations with him when he left the office that fateful Friday,
unnoticed by Frye and Haddock. But if he had taken the
examinations with him, they should be in the briefcase that
had been found with him in the car.

6

FRANCIS LIFTED HIS EYEBROWS expressively when Maggie went by his desk and into the presidential office. Greg was behind the desk. He looked as if he hadn't yet sat down. He looked as if he might never sit down again. Maggie closed the door behind her, crossed the room, and took him in her arms.

"What is it?"

She had pinned his arms, and he had difficulty waving the tabloid in explanation. Of course, she already knew what had upset him.

"Tell me one story that was in the *News* last week," she said.

"What the hell does that mean?"

"These things loom large for the moment of their existence. Then they are totally forgotten."

"They why do we pay Farkas so much money trying to get the place mentioned by the news media?"

"That's a question to put to Farkas rather than me. Had coffee?"

Calmness is all. What a boy he was after all. Twelve years older than she was, yet she felt like a mother, a grandmother, to him. Most of the things he took her advice on were matters he understood far better than she did. She had discovered that a firm, confident manner went a long way with Greg. She buzzed Francis, told him to bring in coffee, and got Greg seated in a presidential way behind the desk.

If a sensational story in a tabloid affected him this way, he would really unravel if Joyce found out about them. Something was bound to happen, sooner or later, of course. Maggie could not believe her ears when Greg told her of discussing the matter with Priscilla.

"With your driver!"

"You'd have to know Priscilla better."

She couldn't blame the driver; it was Greg's stupidity. How had the man ever been elected to Congress? How had he ever been named president even of a college as low on the totem pole as LBJ? Her own speaking with Priscilla had been, Maggie conceded, a mistake. But apparently the driver hadn't mentioned it to Greg in one of their democratic chats on the way to the office. Finding out about the student Priscilla was going with gave her clout, and Maggie had thought it would be enough. As Greg said, you'd have to know Priscilla.

"You're lecturing me about love affairs?" Pinched little face, tough broad manner, she seemed to have had a male chauffeur's suit tailored to fit her, more or less. When had she last worn a skirt? If Maggie's information about Priscilla and Roy Hastings had not come from Haddock, always an unimpeachable source when it came to sexual antics, she would have thought Priscilla and Stella Houston might get along. Did Haddock know about her and Greg? To ask the question was to answer it. Of course he did. But then, Maggie did not have the same interest in keeping it a big dark secret.

"I just wanted you to know your big dark secret isn't a secret anymore," she'd said to Priscilla.

The thin-lipped mouth opened in disbelief. A racist remark from the dean?

"You ever been married, Priss?"

The chauffeur suggested an impossible feat involving the dean's reproductive organs. Vulgarity always gave the recipient an edge. Maggie knew from long experience how her ability to remain unruffled ruffled others. Priscilla was no exception. But she had not been ruffled enough to run to Greg about it. Even so, Maggie considered the exchange a mistake. She had conveyed the damaging information that she cared enough about it to want to shut Priscilla up. She told herself she was only thinking of Greg, but that was not wholly true. The thought of this bony little broad advising Greg about his relations with her angered Maggie.

If talking to Priscilla had been a mistake, telling Greg about his driver's affair had been right. It should provide him protection during the drives to and from work.

"Where did the paper get all this information, Maggie?" Calmer now, Greg indicated the tabloid he had cast aside.

"August Frye."

"Frye!"

"Larry Gridiron can tell you all about it. August got in touch with a former student, now a police detective, and told him Stanley Bledsoe had been murdered."

"On what basis?"

"Priscilla's boyfriend."

She reminded him of Roy Hastings and Priscilla, adding something she had recently learned.

"A black student?" He struggled to keep judgment from his voice, but he wasn't fooling Maggie.

"We'll have to wait to see if there's a sequel to the story tomorrow."

"My God! Stay with me while I talk to Farkas."

$\triangledown$

7

WHEN GRIDIRON CALLED MAGGIE'S office again, Haddock said she was still with the president. For the past hour in his office, ever since he had seen that headline on the bus, Gridiron had been rehearsing what he would say to the dean. He wanted to get it over with. He wanted to do it before he lost his nerve and changed his mind. What he wanted to do was make certain August Frye caught hell for this.

In Larry Gridiron's estimation, his old friend August was responsible for the death of young Bledsoe. He had hounded him to the grave. Then he called in the police in the person of James Cable and tried to stir up posthumous trouble as well. It must be tough, sitting in that office, looking at that empty desk, knowing that what he had done had driven Stanley Bledsoe to take his own life.

"Why do you think he committed suicide?" Maxine had asked.

"Do you really think that is the question?" But not even Maxine seemed to understand what a bastard August had been.

"It was a joke, Larry."

"It's no joke for a professor to be accused of plagiarism."

"But August says the letter he drafted would have cleared it all up."

"Maybe. It doesn't matter. He was too late."

August had sat at their dining-room table and fed Maxine a song and dance about students menacing Stanley, claiming to be convinced his office mate had been killed. So when August left, Larry brought up the poem. He had never told Maxine about it. No point in inviting more grief from her. She thought he acted like an undergraduate when he was with August anyway. But perversely, in this instance she took August's side.

"The young man didn't commit suicide, Larry. Wasn't he hit on the head?"

Larry didn't care how Bledsoe did away with himself. The point was that he had. He had been driven to it. Larry was sure of it. August was just trying to deflect guilt from himself—he had done it with Maxine, he had done it with Cable. Now there was this stupid story in the *Daily News*, and Larry Gridiron was determined August would pay the price for stirring up publicity about this tragedy. And he couldn't get to Maggie Downs.

It made him antsy to be there in the office where the phone could ring or someone just come by he couldn't dodge and that would put off even longer his call on Maggie. Mitzi in the outer office and his own closed door should have been protection enough, and normally it was, but Mitzi had a heart of gold. And she was putty in the hands of a fellow black. Thanks to Mitzi, he had wasted something like three hours on the student Roy Hastings. If Mitzi let him in because he was black, Gridiron had treated Hastings's request with a seriousness it didn't deserve.

"I wanna appeal a flunk."

"The semester is still young. You haven't flunked anything."

"This was last year."

"Last year."

"Spring. He flunked me, and I think I passed."

It was an absurd request, but absurdity was no longer ruled out of academe. There had been a time, and Gridiron remembered it well, when a teacher was absolute ruler of his classroom. If he caught you cheating, out you went and that was it. No more. Now the teacher filed a claim that cheating had taken place, and there was a hearing before a committee, one third of whose members were students and one third untenured faculty, the rest senior faculty. Most accusations were turned down by a two-thirds vote, the younger faculty currying favor with the students. One accusing teacher whose claim had been voted down was subsequently sued in civil court for libel and slander, and it had been touch and go before he was acquitted. Accusations of cheating had all but ceased. Grades had been the last bastion, and even they were threatened by the appeal process narrowly passed by the faculty senate two years ago. Because of grade inflation, appeals usually aimed at upping C's to B's or B's to A's, and so far the *ad hoc* committees appointed had ruled in favor of the professor. But Gridiron could all too easily imagine the day when any grade less than an A would be appealed and most appeals granted. By that time he hoped to be vegetating in the Arizona sunshine. So Roy Hastings was anomalous in two respects. First, he had actually managed to receive a failing grade at Lyndon Johnson. Second, he had waited past the statutory time to protest it and demand a hearing. Gridiron should have sent him on his way.

"I'll look into it," he said. "What course was it?"

"The Novel."

"Professor?"

"Bledsoe."

Gridiron stopped writing and looked up at Hastings. He looked like Mr. Clean except that he was black. No expression, eyes so folded in flesh it was hard to read them. He put down his ballpoint.

"Professor Bledsoe is dead."

A little silence. "He flunked me."

"I understand. But he's dead now."

"I'm not. He flunked me. I want it changed."

"I'll look into it."

He got up and walked into the outer office with Hastings. Did he want Mitzi to look up and see the nice chairperson being especially nice to a black student? He actually shook hands with Hastings. Back behind his own closed door, he asked himself what was becoming of him. Last spring or not, he should have told Hastings he wouldn't initiate the appeals process on a failure. Maybe he had no choice on that, but he did when the student had waited this long. And with a deceased professor! Were Bledsoe's marks subject to posthumous change? That was ridiculous.

Ridiculous or not, he had called August and asked if Bledsoe's grade book was in the office.

"His grade book?"

"Let me know if you find it."

August came to see him ten minutes later.

"Find it?"

He stood on one leg and looked down at Gridiron. "Is it Roy Hastings?"

"You know the student?"

"Larry, that's the big guy who was intimidating Stanley. That's the student who flunked the course last year and signed up again and informed Stanley that this time he was going to pass. That was a threat."

"He wants to appeal the fail."

Gridiron was prepared for the worst. He was putting himself in August's hands, inviting the withering remarks he knew must be forming on his colleague's tongue. But August said nothing of a critical kind. Nothing at all.

"The grade book is not in the office." August spoke carefully. Larry was sure that, if he was not lying, August was telling him a partial truth. He could have hugged him.

"Thanks, August."

Within ten minutes, his gratitude had turned to renewed hatred. For August to have said nothing about his craven willingness to consider tinkering with Bledsoe's grades was unforgivable. Gridiron knew what August must think of him. What he thought of himself. He had been in office only weeks, and already it had corrupted him. He had conferred on August the right to patronize him, to look down from a lofty height and not even show him the respect of criticism.

Such thoughts whetted his appetite to blow the whistle on August now over the *Daily News* story. He dialed the dean's office again.

"When the hell will she be back?" he asked Haddock.

"You could just go to Hackis's office if it's about the *Daily News*. That's what they're talking about."

Good idea. It was a lot better than stewing in his office, having imaginary conversations, building the indictment against August. On the way to Hackis's office, he asked himself what he expected them to do to August. This slowed his step. But not for long. If all they did was scold August, he would be happy. Scold him and see him for what he really was, not good old August Frye, the senior member of the English Department, everyone's friend, everyone's idea of the wise old professor. Ha. Tell it to Stanley Bledsoe.

Francis Ceascu, assistant to the president, pink plaid shirt, red tie, pale-blue suit, gave a little nod and smile when Gridiron came into his office as if the chairperson of English were doing precisely what Francis wished him to do.

"I was just about to call you."

"Is Maggie still here?"

"The dean is with the president, yes. Dr. Hackis wishes to see you."

Doctor Hackis! Hackis and his counterpart at a community college in Detroit had traded honorary doctorates, and ever since Francis used the sobriquet as if Hackis had received the Nobel Prize.

"The *Daily News*?"

A pained expression. "I never read it, of course. If I ever wondered why, I no longer do. My advice is call in counsel and sue."

"What did Hackis say to that?"

"He has not yet asked for my advice."

Francis knocked, opened the door, and stepped aside.

Gridiron walked in. Hackis was seated behind his desk; Maggie was standing behind him. Facing them, on his feet, was Farkas, the PR man, his belly rolling over his belt, scruffy hair mussed from constant combing with his fingers, his mouth a blur as he talked. Maggie pointed to a chair facing the desk. Gridiron sat and had to listen to ten minutes of drivel.

"So that's it. A special convocation. We announce the pledge taken by administration, staff, and faculty to sell any stocks and bonds they now own in companies doing business with South Africa. The Kenyan ambassador to the U.N., escorted by a dozen dean's list blacks, male and female, is given an honorary doctorate of humane letters. You read the citation but depart from the text to eulogize the ambassador. Both citation and departure will be provided the media. No local channel will pass it by, and the network stations may get it into national newscasts. Result? We bury the *Daily News* in a snowstorm of favorable coverage."

Hackis nodded approval all through this. Gridiron's eye met Maggie's. They averted their gazes simultaneously.

"What do you say, Maggie?"

"It's worked everywhere else it's been tried."

"Hey," Farkas protested. "Lay off. This is original."

"Well, a variation on an original."

Hackis clearly did not appreciate the dean's reaction. He looked at Gridiron.

"What's your advice, Larry?"

"Have you thought of calling in counsel and suing?"

Maggie laughed. Farkas laughed. After a moment, Hackis laughed.

"And prolong it, Larry?" Farkas asked, shaking his head. "Not smart. You don't put out a fire by fueling it."

Being laughed at by the dean and president was bad enough, but to be corrected by Farkas! Only a month ago, this would have been unthinkable or if thought of would have demanded a dramatic response, like resigning. Gridiron looked at Farkas.

"You're right," he said.

8

H<small>E WAS UNABLE TO</small> reach Cable until late that afternoon, having spent most of the day preoccupied with the thought of the missing blue books. His lecture on Milton would have surprised anyone knowledgeable in the poet's work. From time to time, Frye interested himself. His lecture, a counterpart of automatic writing, produced several remarks that might actually make sense if pursued. One of the more sobering aspects of teaching at LBJ was the realization that one could get away with murder in the classroom, say anything with impunity. It was a very corrupting position to be in; anything one said was accepted as gospel truth. As long as it concerned literature, that is. Any remark that questioned the antinomian prejudices of the day was sure to waken the slumbering beast and he would be bombarded with illiterate but passionate proclamations. Frye had learned to couch his animadversions in safely historical terms.

"No examination booklets in the briefcase," Cable said after consulting the list. "What about them?"

August explained what had prompted him to look for the exams.

"Maybe they're in his apartment."

"Should I find out?"

"You're the one who thinks they're important," Cable said.

"Don't you?"

"They'll be a lot more important if you can't find them."

It was a daunting prospect to face Bledsoe senior again. He had sat mute in a folding chair at the funeral service, taking no noticeable interest in the urn of his son's ashes. His deafness made him almost autistic. How could such a man live alone?

When he arrived in the Bronx, Frye went immediately to the super's apartment. The blast of discordant noise from behind the closed door told him the man was in. The door was unlocked. He opened it and looked in. Norman, the ponytailed super, eyes closed, barefoot, was gyrating to the weird rhythms of the music. Frye pulled the door shut. The super would be deaf before he was half Mr. Bledsoe's age.

He climbed to the floor where Bledsoe had lived and pounded and shouted in the way he had been taught. Two other tenants looked out at him over door chains, then shut themselves in again. After ten minutes of pounding, Mr. Bledsoe opened his door a crack.

Something like recognition shone in his eyes. He closed the door, loosened the chain, then opened to his late son's senior colleague.

Roy Hastings sat on the couch.

Behind Frye, Mr. Bledsoe was fussing with the chain. From the couch the huge student looked up at him expressionlessly. Among the thoughts that went through August Frye's mind was that no one knew he had come here. He should have waited and caught Norman's attention. Dear God, if only Norman had come up with him. Now here he was alone with a deaf old man and the murderer of Stanley Bledsoe.

Hastings patted the couch beside him.

Frye stepped back, bumping into Mr. Bledsoe. The old man grinned and threw out his hands in apology.

"This is one of Stanley's students," the old man piped.

"Yes, I know." He turned to Roy. "What are you doing here?"

"He can't hear you," Roy said.

"How does he know who you are?"

"Stanley never spoke much of his students," Mr. Bledsoe said.

"I want that exam book."

"I never even knew Stanley had a secretary," the old man said in marveling tones.

August turned to the old man, and that is when he saw the woman. Apparently, she had been somewhere down that long hallway that led away from the living room. She ignored August, lifted her hands, and moved her fingers rapidly.

"This is Stanley's friend. Another professor," Mr. Bledsoe said to her.

Her hands moved again. She looked like an inept magician, trying to mesmerize him. August realized it was sign language. She had used it to lie her way in here. Stanley's secretary!

"Who are you?"

"Professor who?"

"Did you tell Mr. Bledsoe you were his son's secretary?"

"Frye," Hastings said. "He's in the same office as Bledsoe."

"I'm sorry, I don't remember your name," Mr. Bledsoe said softly to August.

"I think I found them," the woman said to Roy, and he put his hands on his knees and levered himself to his feet. The woman disappeared down the hall, and Roy followed her.

August took the old man by the arms and looked directly into his eyes. He moved his mouth in exaggerated articulateness, not saying the words aloud. What was the use?

"She is not Stanley's secretary."

Mr. Bledsoe was looking directly at his lips.

"Se-cre-tary," August enunciated, and shook his head from side to side.

But the old man, getting the word, beamed, bobbing his head up and down.

"She came for some papers."

August's eyes drifted to the door. The chain. He stepped around Mr. Bledsoe and reached for the chain, but before he could slide it free a huge black hand closed over his.

"Where you going?" Hastings asked.

"Let go of my hand!"

In response, Hastings increased the pressure as he led August to the couch. "Sit down."

The woman was carrying an armful of blue books. She sat next to August, bumping against him. "Move over."

He got to his feet.

"Sit down," Roy said.

Mr. Bledsoe sat in a rocker that was angled to face the television set, smiling at each of his guests in turn. August sat at the end of the couch closest to the old man. He felt contemporary with Stanley's father, two old men no one would care to harm. He rubbed the hand Roy had crushed, because it hurt, and to emphasize that he was fragile and old. Roy sat on the other side of the woman, and they began to look through the blue books. She just sailed them onto the floor after looking at them.

"Pick them up," she said.

Hastings did not move and she repeated the command, more sharply. Then she looked at August. She was speaking to him! He turned away, unwilling to dignify her demand with an answer.

"You want Roy to crack your knuckles some more, then don't pick them up."

August got on his knees and began to pick up the blue books. He felt like weeping. Why had he come on this fool's errand? Even as he picked up blue books, others fluttered to the floor. He no longer believed that eventually these two would go, leaving two old men behind.

"That's one," Roy said.

"How many are there?"

"I don't remember."

"Geez."

August looked up at Mr. Bledsoe. The old man was smiling at him, as if they were all engaged in a game. Was he senile as well as deaf? There was no indication that he found anything taking place in the apartment strange. Perhaps it was so unusual an event, he could only enjoy it. How long had it been since anyone other than his son was in this apartment? For some time now he had been here all alone. Why, this was like a holiday, a party.

"Here's another for you," the woman said, tossing another blue book at him.

On his knees, feeling worse than he had since Grace died, August wondered about this strange couple. There were many mixed couples at Lyndon Johnson, but these two were a mismatch. Roy, huge, stupid, powerful; the woman a little wiry bitch with brains enough for both of them. What good were those damned blue books? She must understand they weren't worth all this trouble. The thought continued. They weren't worth killing for.

Had Stanley died because he flunked that monster on the couch? Hastings should never have been admitted to college, not even Lyndon Johnson. It was a travesty of education. Could he threaten his way to a degree? Why not? August Frye, picking up blue books from the Bledsoe floor, eyes blurred with tears. This is what old Romans must have felt when his barbaric ancestors descended on the eternal city and put out the light of learning. He wanted to curse Stanley for standing up for principle and failing Hastings, but what he felt instead was grudging admiration for his office mate.

Mr. Bledsoe got up from his rocker and came to August. He tried to kneel down. "I'll help you," he said.

Having found what they came for, Roy and the woman were on their feet. "C'mon, pop," she said, leading Mr. Bledsoe to his rocker. Hastings took August's arm and jerked him to his feet. He lost his hold on the blue books and they fluttered to the floor. August looked at Hastings, waiting for the command to pick the booklets up again.

"Bring him along," the woman said, and Hastings pushed August toward the door. He twisted free and got seated on the couch again, his arms behind him so Hastings could not grab them.

"I'll stay with Mr. Bledsoe." He smiled at the old man, who smiled back.

"I think you better come with us, Frye," the woman said.

"Why?"

"Who knows what you'll tell the old guy about us?"

"But he can't hear me!"

"Then why do you want to stay?"

"Come on," Roy said, reaching for him.

August squirmed into the corner of the couch. The woman was moving her fingers again, and the old man followed them. He began to frown. He glanced at August, then back at the hands. His expression became angry.

"I want you to leave my home," he said to August.

"What did you tell him?" he demanded, his voice rising. Roy had got a grip on one of his arms and pulled him up. "These two killed Stanley! They killed your son!"

All movement stopped, silence fell. Roy released his arm, but a moment later August's ear exploded. He reeled, losing his balance, stumbling toward the woman. She stepped aside to let him fall.

"You're crazy," she said to August. "Do you know that?"

He looked up at her with hatred.

There was the sound of the chain as Roy took it off the door. He said to August, "Let's go."

"I won't!"

"The man wants you out of his house. You heard him."

The woman was using sign language again. Mr. Bledsoe rose from his rocker and glared at August. "You get out of here. Now!"

The only thing that enabled him to leave the apartment was the thought that below were people who could hear him if he shouted. Below was Norman the superintendent. The woman went first, then August, then Hastings. Mr. Bledsoe stood in his doorway, waving his hand, sorry to see them go. Except for August Frye, of course. What had they told the old man to make him glare so angrily at him?

On the way down, August thought ahead. Four flights would bring them into the little lobby. There a door was closed on the stairs leading down to Norman's apartment. He would dash for the door, pull it shut after him, and just rush into Norman's apartment. Whether or not these two pursued him, he would be safe once he got the superintendent's attention.

When they reached the landing of the second floor and started down the final flight, August felt suffused with hope. In a few moments, he would be free of these two. Halfway down this flight, the woman stopped and looked up at him.

"We're going to walk straight out the door and to the street. There is a car there. Tell me you're not going to make a fuss."

He made a face. Who, me? Leave when we're having so much fun?

"Say it," she said, and Roy's hand descended on his shoulder.

"Okay. I won't make a fuss."

"See that you don't."

She continued on down, and August followed, full of doubt now but determined to try to get to the superintendent. The woman kept going toward the front entrance when she reached the lobby. August took two steps after her then turned and dashed to the closed door. He got it open and pulled it shut after him. No key to turn and lock it. He scrambled down the short flight, hand lifted to pound on the door as he turned its handle.

He hit the door twice and turned the handle and pushed. It was locked! Roy was coming after him. August, crying in frustration, kicked at the door several times before Hastings grabbed him and pushed him spinning toward the stairway. He put out his hands to cushion his fall. The woman stood in the doorway, looking down at him with a cruel smile on her face.

"You lied," she said.

Roy got him to his feet and propelled him up the stairs and right across the lobby to where the woman held the door open. Beyond the door was the normalcy of a city street. August brushed past her and then broke for freedom, running zigzag up the street, shouting at the top of his lungs.

▽

9

HEALY IN THE BRONX kept him in the picture—Healy's phrase—but Cable began to think the college was where the explanation of Bledsoe's death would be found, even though he had died in the Bronx. The car registration in the name of Priscilla Cortez of Brooklyn was just a fact to Healy, and this was all it seemed to Cable, too, until he went to Brooklyn and talked with her.

She was a little bantamweight with short hair and side-of-the-mouth delivery she seemed to work on. Tough. If she weren't a woman, you'd say macho. Meaning she wasn't mucho woman.

"God, not again" was her reaction when he flashed his shield and said he wanted to talk about the car. "I thought when I sold it I wouldn't be bothered any more."

"Who's been bothering you?"

"If I knew I was this important, I would have had my car stolen long ago."

"A dead man was found in your car."

"Just because they steal them doesn't mean they can drive them." She fitted a cigarette into the corner of her mouth and went to work on a Zippo. Cable waited until she got it going; it took a dozen tries, leaving her thumb all gray.

"I see you're a chauffeur."

She nodded as she inhaled deeply.

"What company do you work for?"

They were standing in the hallway of the building, and Cable's varicose veins were throbbing painfully.

"I don't. I drive for an executive."

"Tell me about it."

"About driving?" She decided to be annoyed rather than funny, and pushed away from the wall. "What does where I work have to do with my car gets stolen?"

"You'd be surprised."

"Look, I don't want my employer brought into this. Why should he be? My car was here in Brooklyn, I work in Manhattan, it was found in the Bronx."

"I'm not a reporter, miss. I'm a cop. You can tell me who you work for."

She resisted for several minutes more, ensuring that Cable would not drop it, though that could not have been her intention.

"He's an educator."

"What's that mean? A teacher?"

"That's close enough."

"A teacher who can afford a private chauffeur? I'd like to know more about her."

"It's a man." This seemed important to her. But it was when she mentioned Lyndon Johnson that, as Healy would say, the penny dropped.

"You drive for Hackis?"

"You know him?"

"Not really. You say you sold the car?"

"I never said that."

Cable had made the transition because he knew he had found out something important, but it wasn't until an hour and a half later, having tailed her from Brooklyn and watched her meet an obviously waiting young black of enormous size, that he was certain that Lyndon Johnson Community College was where the riddle would be solved.

The young black was waiting for her in the Port Authority

terminal. She looked about a fourth his size as she rubbed against him and tried unsuccessfully to elicit an affectionate response from him. Cable thought this guy's idea of foreplay would be turning out the lights first. Priscilla Cortez was doing the talking, but he wasn't listening. Was he as stupid as he looked?

The couple stood in the flow of traffic, forcing people to detour around them, squeeze by, push through as best they could. Over by the lockers, Cable was letting things combine freely in his mind. Cortez was President Hackis's driver, the dead body found in her car was that of Professor Stanley Bledsoe. She knew that. She couldn't expect him to believe that a college professor was a car thief, particularly of battered Volkswagen bugs like hers. And then he remembered the story August Frye had told him of Bledsoe's menacing student. A big black kid who had flunked and didn't like it. Priscilla's friend fit the description.

She seemed to be trying to talk reason to him, but he looked blankly over her head and when she was done said something that made her shake her head and, he would bet, swear. Finally, she gave up. They worked against the stream of traffic into the street, where she hailed a cab while he waited on the curb. He had won the argument, but she was running the show. Priscilla Cortez would always want to be in charge, Cable thought.

He walked up the street and intercepted a cab before he could see Priscilla wave.

"Don't start yet," he told the driver. "I want you to follow those two when they get a cab."

The impatient look went when the driver turned to see his shield.

"What have they done?"

"Jaywalked."

"No kidding."

"It's police harassment."

The cabbie tried to grin, but he was out of practice.

When Priscilla and her man caught a cab, they went to

the Bronx. Cable tried to keep his mind a blank. They might have been determined to substantiate his suspicion. Sure enough, the cab pulled up in front of the building in which Stanley Bledsoe had lived. They stood for a moment on the curb where the car in which Bledsoe's body had been found was parked. Cable let his cab go after the couple entered the building. He took up his station on the street across from the entrance.

Twenty minutes later August Frye showed up, a short dumpy figure, topcoat flapping, bald head rising from the wind-tossed white fringe. Cable half turned away, but it was obvious Frye was impervious to the world. He had a destination, and all his attention was on it. He plunged into the entrance of the Bledsoe building. Cable, not taking his eyes from the entrance, went unthinkingly to the corner, where he bought a package of cigarettes and for the first time in seven and a half years lit one up. He had smoked three of them before he remembered that he no longer smoked. He had three more while he waited. Smoking seemed called for somehow, but it was an activity wholly contained in this event. He did not feel that he had taken it up again. He didn't think of it much at all at the time. His eye was on that entrance. What he thought about was whether or not it was wise to have decided to wait outside rather than go right in and see what the hell those three were doing calling on old Mr. Bledsoe.

The woman came out first, and then came Frye, pushed outside by the big black who came right after him. Frye wasn't wearing the topcoat he'd had on going in, and his side hair looked wilder than before. He looked desperately around and then began to run up the street. Not fast, his knees pumped, his head went back, he wasn't exactly running in place, but he didn't get far from the black. The fellow was on him in a minute and that was when Cable started across the street, his weapon drawn, shouting at the big guy to freeze.

He froze. He stood obediently against the wall while Cable

frisked him. Frye seemed to be weeping; Priscilla wanted to know what the hell he was doing in the Bronx. Cable got the cuffs on the man.

"That's what we're going to talk about. You want to be arrested before or after?"

"Arrested for what!"

"Never return to the scene of the crime. That's Rule One."

Her fury made up for the big guy's docility. Even with the cuffs on, he checked to make sure the booklets sticking out of his pocket were still there.

"Thank God you came," August Frye said, gripping his arm.

A witness called the police, and thus it was in a Bronx precinct that Cable questioned Priscilla Cortez and Roy Hastings. August Frye had returned to the Bledsoe apartment, suggesting that someone who knew sign language accompany him, but the police countered with the advice that he write things out for Mr. Bledsoe.

"I never thought of that."

Hastings and Cortez were kept separated, and Cable and Healy alternated between the two.

"What the hell for?" Priscilla demanded when told she could and should contact a lawyer.

"Aw, c'mon. Roy may be stupid, but you're not."

"He's not stupid!"

"I looked at the blue books. He thinks they contain good work. He's stupid."

"How the hell would you know?"

"Is that what you were after up there, the blue books? How'd you know they were there?"

The answer to the first question was obviously yes, though she did not admit it until the following morning. That was when she decided that, despite appearances, Cable was her friend.

"You have to know it all," she said. "It only makes sense when you know the whole story."

"That's what I'm here for. More coffee?"

The whole story was this. Roy had an obsession about passing Bledsoe's course. He wanted his exam booklet. Bledsoe had told him it was okay, but Roy wanted to see it. That was when she acted dumber than Roy, agreeing that they should lean on Bledsoe and get the blue book. Even as she said it, Priscilla seemed to find it hard to believe that she had gone along with Roy's obsession.

"We waited until Bledsoe came out of the building his office is in, and I called to him. The passenger door was open, and he came over, and Roy, who was in the back, reached out and pulled him inside."

"Bledsoe was in the passenger seat, you're driving, Hastings is in back?"

"That's right."

They drove around, because after Bledsoe understood what they wanted he turned tough. Threats didn't bother him. Priscilla thought this was because he could look at her, not Roy. But there was something eerie in his attitude, as if he didn't give a damn about anything. Roy squeezed his shoulder a bit and he cried out, but that was all.

"We'll go back to your office and look around," Priscilla suggested, making a turn.

Bledsoe laughed. Really laughed. The exam booklets weren't in his office. From the back Roy asked if they were at home. Priscilla was looking at Bledsoe then, and his expression gave him away. Roy had the address in the Bronx.

Priscilla stopped, sipped her coffee, stuck out a brown tongue, and crossed her eyes. "This is my last cup."

Her explanation of how Bledsoe died was simple. And plausible. Distracted by everything going on in the car, she had slammed on the brakes at a red light.

"He just dipped forward and hit his head with a kind of bonk. That was all. He even sat back again when the car came to a stop. We didn't know anything was wrong at first. Not until he wouldn't answer and didn't squawk when Roy applied pressure. I pulled over. No pulse. He was dead."

She could have made it up, but the way she reacted when

he expressed incredulity rang true. Maybe Roy had pushed Bledsoe forward in an effort to persuade him? She shook her head.

"It happened the way I said."

What to do with a dead body in her car? She drove on to Bledsoe's, parked the car in front of the building. That's when Roy bolted, not liking the thought of being in the same car as a dead man.

"I went after him, after locking the car." A wry smile. "Did I think someone would steal the body?"

"You left the motor running."

She looked at him, but he could see she was reconstructing the events of that fateful day.

"The ignition was on, Priscilla. The tank was empty."

"Jesus." She sat back. "It's a good thing he was already dead."

"Why?"

"I've been having trouble with the exhaust. It seeps into the car. I always drove with the window open."

"The windows were closed."

"I closed them when I locked the car."

She waited for him to say more. It was possible that it had happened as she said. She could have forgotten the motor in her eagerness to corral Roy before he got away. Besides, she had assumed they would be going back to the car. Roy talked her into just leaving it. There was no way they could explain the body to the cops. The next day, she reported her car missing. That was it.

Cable believed her. But they are more skeptical in the Bronx.

"It's all a bunch of shit," Healy decided, and held them over.

10

WHATEVER ONE THOUGHT OF Farkas's idea of a special convocation to confer an honorary degree on the Kenyan ambassador to the U.N., etc., etc., it took time to arrange. Too much time, as it turned out. The arrest the following day of Priscilla Cortez and Roy Hastings, with the accusing August Frye at center stage, made the first story in the *Daily News* look like a Farkas press release by comparison.

"I'll take care of it," Maggie told Greg.

"How?" He sat on the edge of the bed, smoking a smokeless cigarette, running his fingers through his red hair, a Farkas habit. He had just expressed hope that Farkas would have another inspiration.

"First, I'm getting you out of here."

"This was your idea."

Gallantry is not dead. Sometimes Maggie yearned for the Spencer Tracy/Katharine Hepburn world in which men were nice to women. "You should have known better."

She had brought him to her apartment to shore him up. The arrests coming on top of the first news story threatened to unglue him, and it was important to keep him out of the way of reporters. That had been Farkas's concern, leaving the means to her. Not even a smirk. There'd better not be. Farkas loved to meet the press. A briefing provided a ritualistic occasion to lie and be lied to, and everyone knew it. Bringing Hackis home hadn't helped. She should have left him to Joyce.

Imagine what that bitch would say to Greg when he did get home. Maggie believed Greg when he said Joyce took delight in the trouble the *Daily News* story threatened. Does every wife secretly seek her husband's downfall? With Joyce it was no secret.

Maggie literally waved a hand to dismiss such thoughts. She would not see herself in relation to Greg's wife. Joyce was his problem, not hers. But the crescendoing scandal of Stanley Bledsoe's death was everybody's problem. A point she tried to bring home to August Frye when she returned to her office later that afternoon.

He sat on the other side of her desk, blinking at her, letting the silence build before saying, "I can't believe what I have just heard."

"That's as may be, August. Perhaps you heard something other than what I said. My point is that it is to the advantage of all of us to get these matters out of the newspapers and off television." Crews from local channels were tripping over one another on campus, in the hallways of buildings. August Frye had been interviewed in his office, the camera drifting ghoulishly to the empty desk Professor Stanley Bledsoe had recently occupied and would occupy no more.

"You want to hush this up."

"No. But I do not want it magnified. That is not the same thing."

"Maggie, this is not a matter of public relations. We are talking of a colleague and friend. . . . "

"I watched your interview, August."

That stopped him, but at a price. He stood, a medium-sized, overweight, bald old man, perhaps, but her remark had conferred moral authority on him. She might be callous if she chose; he would honor the memory of a promising young colleague.

He bumped into the incoming Gridiron on his way out of

her office, and Maggie was surprised by their lack of cordiality with one another. And indeed Gridiron let her know what he thought of August Frye naming himself chief mourner for Stanley. He told her of the Henry VIII poem.

"Henry VIII wrote poetry? When did he have time?"

"Stanley was devastated by the wire from the magazine. Plagiarism. Imagine. August Frye is acting out of the guilt he feels for that. Whatever the details of Stanley's death, August bears a share of responsibility, and he knows it."

Interesting, perhaps, and she could have used it a few minutes earlier as repartee, but she was not looking for new ways of prolonging morbid interest in Stanley Bledsoe. Stella Houston was demanding that the college put its counsel and legal staff at the disposal of Priscilla and Roy.

"Their problems have nothing to do with Lyndon Johnson," Maggie replied.

"Of course they do. She drives Hackis and he is enrolled as a student and their problems connect with poor Stanley."

"They are charged with falsely reporting a stolen car and failing to report a fatal accident. I don't think anyone expects those charges to be pursued. What is needed is a decent interval of neglect so it can all fade away."

At least Stella had not pretended to moral outrage. Predictably, her concern was Priscilla Cortez. She had spoken with the spunky chauffeur and professed to see in her one version of the woman of tomorrow.

"You may be right," Maggie said, not finding the prospect as pleasant as Stella apparently did. "But asking Ciappi's office to get involved in these minor charges is, if I may say so, ridiculous. Quite apart from the fact that Ciappi would likely regard it as an improper use of college funds."

Gridiron, she realized, expected her to be shocked beyond belief at what August Frye had done. Maggie found it funny, sending a poem of Henry VIII's to a journal and having it accepted. That fit in with her generally contemptuous attitude toward the humanities in general. To her unexpressed surprise, Gridiron seemed almost to want charges brought against August Frye.

And so the tempest swirled, out of the teapot of Lyndon Johnson College, into the columns of newspapers and televised local news, a minor item in the bad news of the world, perhaps, but major enough to disrupt for days the business of the college. And Maggie was at the eye of the storm, acutely aware that her function was to be the lightning rod that drew to itself and away from Greg Hackis and the school's reputation the sputtering flashes of damaging electricity. Greg was not grateful, and everyone else seemed to resent her efforts to diminish the damage to Lyndon Johnson. There had been a time when this would have depressed her and made her feel sorry for herself, but now she relished it. She liked to feel that she alone kept her head while all her colleagues, allegedly intellectuals, went up in emotional smoke. Including Haddock.

It was with this self-satisfying attitude that, at day's end, she got into the elevator to descend to the garage and her car, preoccupied, aware of others in the elevator, not really taking notice. The elevator rocked in the shaft in its usual annoying way, making her aware of her surroundings. She looked up at the mirrored ceiling of the elevator. An unthinking exposure of her throat. It was the last deed she performed. The movement reflected in the ceiling alarmed her too late. Something enclosed her throat, a terrible pressure was applied and pain radiated through her body as she dropped painfully into the waiting darkness.

PART THREE

▽

Improper Names

$\triangledown$

1

LARRY GRIDIRON DID NOT drive a car to work. He did not own a car. A car was a nuisance rather than a convenience in Manhattan. Normally he left the Arts & Letters building by the west exit onto Second Avenue. He almost never left by way of the garage in the basement of the building. But today he had taken the stairs to the garage level because a janitor was swabbing the main lobby.

That was the first in a chain of unintended, unlooked-for events.

He pushed through the door and confronted a sea of parked automobiles. Where the hell was the exit ramp? Skating across the wet lobby above would have been better than this. Cursing, he wandered among the cars seeking a way out. The ramp up which cars went to the street was at the far west end. Larry started toward it, then stopped. It didn't seem very smart to walk up a narrow ramp designed for automobiles. He had a pedestrian's wariness of speeding cars, and he had seen the recklessness with which motorists entered and left garages. The hell with it. He decided to take the elevator back to the lobby.

The elevator was in use, but he punched the button anyway, wondering what his chances were that the elevator would stop on the first floor and be immediately commandeered by someone going up. Half a minute went by, and he decided to correct his mistake and return the way he had come. The stairway. Larry's hand was on the doorknob when he heard the elevator door open. He darted among the cars, hurrying back to it. When he rounded the pillar, he accelerated. The door of the elevator was still open.

It remained open. Something prevented it from closing. A body, a woman's body. She lay half in, half out of the car. Gridiron warily approached to see what the matter was. And then he recognized her. Maggie Downs!

When he remembered later that his first thought was to run back to the stairway and get out of there, he wished he had. The suggestion had probably been made by his guardian angel. Get the hell out of here. This is trouble.

But he had already crouched to see what was wrong with Maggie. He was no judge of whether she was dead or alive, but his instant lay opinion was that Maggie Downs was no more. A bell began to ring, an alarm triggered by the immobility of the elevator. He started to pull Maggie free from the car but stopped. There was an emergency phone in the elevator. He picked it up and in a strangled voice he did not recognize summoned help.

He stayed on during the subsequent hullabaloo. He had no choice. He was the one who had found the body. The corpse, as it turned out, the paramedics trying a number of extraordinary ways to resuscitate Maggie before admitting that she was beyond the reach of their ministrations. The first several times Larry told his story it still held interest for him, but it soon began to cloy and he was able to give a crisp abbreviated version. Was everything really this random, or did the police and medical examiners and paramedics compare what he had said for discrepancies? Long before Cable arrived, Gridiron had the unwelcome feeling that some skepticism greeted his account.

"Did you see anyone else?" Cable asked, lighting a cigarette.

Gridiron sighed. "I won't tell you how often I've answered that question."

"These things quickly turn boring. Did you?"

"I was on the other side of the elevator, starting up the stairs."

"And you changed your mind when you heard the elevator door open."

"That's right."

"What else did you hear?"

"As soon as I heard the door open, I ran around to catch the elevator."

"Seeing no one else."

The trouble with such persistent questioning was that you began to think you ought to be able to give the desired answer. Had he in peripheral vision seen a figure? The answer was still no.

"I can see how someone could hide seconds after getting off the elevator. All he had to do was duck behind a car. But not to make a sound. . . . "

"I wasn't looking for anyone else or listening for any sounds. I was concentrating on getting the elevator."

"You had to realize that it was brought down here by someone."

"No. I had pressed the call button."

"What were you doing in the garage?"

Truth had such a weaselly look when repeated. He had come to the basement because the lobby upstairs was being mopped. Cable just looked at him as if expecting more. It could not be called silence in that echoing garage, but James said nothing more for a full minute.

"Who showed up first?"

"After I called? The guard. Eddie. Then Haddock."

"Who's he?"

"Assistant dean."

"Tell me everything that happened after you sounded the alarm."

"Oh, my God."

The recent past proved to be elusive when he attempted to reconstruct it in chronological order. Eddie came down before the ambulance arrived, and then people in the building who wondered what the hell had gone wrong with the elevator came down to the basement when they heard.

"Ghouls," Haddock had commented, lighting Larry's cigarette and then his own. People were pressing in on the spot where the body of Maggie Downs was being examined.

The elevator was out of use until it had been gone over, so there was a steady traffic on the stairs. Those with cars parked in the garage had a difficult time getting out of there that night. But the sound of motors starting and the rising level of fumes were a feature of the occasion.

"Come down to the precinct with me, Professor Gridiron. It will be best to get this down while it is still fresh."

"Now?"

James Cable looked apologetic, but it was clearly stronger than a mere suggestion.

"I have to call my wife." He glanced at his watch. It was nearly eight o'clock. "My God."

Maxine took it all calmly. She said she hadn't prepared much of a dinner anyway, no trouble. There was the murmur of television in the background, and she spoke in a preoccupied way, the voice of one watching a program while pretending to pay attention to a conversation.

"I've been arrested."

"Hmmm."

"They gave me one phone call, but I wanted to talk to you rather than a lawyer."

"Mmmmm?"

"With any luck I'll be out on parole in a few years and . . ."

"Larry, what on earth are you talking about?"

"Maggie Downs is dead."

"That isn't funny. I'm listening now."

He assured her he was serious. He repeated that he had been asked to go down to the precinct.

"Do you remember James Cable, Maxine?" He turned and looked at Cable as he asked this, but the former student and present detective was not listening. Probably just as well.

Maxine didn't remember him anyway.

"What happened to Maggie?"

"She was assaulted in the elevator. I was there when the elevator opened, and there she was."

Cable was listening now, and Larry could see that he took this version of the story to be out of whack with what he had been saying. He didn't want to go into details, tell Maxine that this had taken place in the basement garage. She knew he didn't drive; why was he in the garage?

"What are you watching?"

"Watching?"

"On television."

"I'm just whiling away the time till you get home."

"Well, while away."

At the precinct he sat beside Cable's desk and spoke slowly while his old student rapidly, with a minimum of fingers, typed out what he said on an old typewriter that stood high on the desk like a collector's item.

$\triangledown$

2

GRIDIRON DID NOT ANSWER at home, at the office of the chair of English, or at the office across the hall from August Frye's. Of course, like other administrators raised from the ranks, August's old friend retained his faculty office as a kind of *memento mori*. Or, at least in Larry's case, the promise of eventual repentance. But Larry was not there, either.

August looked at his living hand upon the dead phone and let the tears run down his cheeks. Alone in his office, unable to reach the one colleague with whom he could discuss in a consoling way the wave of deaths that seemed to be rolling through Lyndon Johnson, August felt like a servant in Job without a Job to report to. I alone have escaped to tell thee.

Even as he wept, he knew his tears were self-indulgent. Did he weep for Maggie Downs, God rest her soul? Did he even weep, as he would like to, for Stanley Bledsoe, also gone to God? In his heart of hearts, he knew that no deep ties of affection bound him to either the dean or his office mate. As Gridiron would be quick to remind him, he had seen Stanley as little more than a source of wry amusement. A young academic hustler, making up in energy what he lacked in soul. Stanley had enough perception to see the poet as the unacknowledged legislator of mankind, but alas not perception enough to see that he himself was no poet.

Then why was he seriously considering editing a posthumous collection of the poems of Stanley Bledsoe for private circulation? As a tribute to his late office mate, that's why. But what kind of tribute was it to a man to parade his lack of talent before posterity? The poems were not worth preserving. August admitted as much.

"Then leave the damned things lie," Larry had said, more impatient than the occasion called for.

"It's a gesture toward the father."

"If he wants to read Stanley's poems, he's got copies, doesn't he?"

August, now a confidant of old Mr. Bledsoe, thanks to endless yellow pages from a legal pad on which he scrawled his inaudible remarks, had been given access to the computer in Stanley's study in the Bronx apartment. What a contrast with his campus office. In their shared office on campus, Stanley had only the Olive Pettigrew Green award and his books to suggest his individuality. At home he worked in a room that contained the layers of his life, the never completely discarded skins of yesteryear. A sateen baseball cap bearing the legend "Bluebirds." A group photo of the team, with Stanley helpfully encircled in ink. August Frye had taken the photograph to the window and studied the narrow face under the bill of the baseball cap. What dreams of glory had disturbed that blank face? The motif of Stanley's room was sports. Every layer of his life involved sports. August Frye could not remember one mention of athletics, except of course of the idiotic jogging. Once Stanley had jogged to school from the Bronx, filling his gasping lungs with all the noxious fumes of the city streets, and then sat huffing and puffing and wringing wet for more than an hour before he was restored enough to change. The marathon pictures and clippings in his Bronx room suggested what might have been his goal.

August Frye would edit Stanley's poems in an ambiguous effort to make at least one major dream of Stanley Bledsoe come true.

Now in his campus office, in the gloaming, going on seven, he dialed once more the Gridiron number and Maxine answered.

"I'm trying to reach Larry."

"They're still talking to him."

"What do you mean?"

"You heard about Maggie, didn't you?"

"Yes."

"Larry was in the garage when the elevator door opened. Her body prevented the door from closing, and that set off the alarm. Larry, like a dummy, called the police. Of course, they think he must have seen the mugger."

"The mugger?"

"Maggie was strangled."

"Good God."

Maxine wanted to wax philosophical about it, lamenting the fragility of life, but August managed to end the conversation. It was important who you discussed such matters with. Where had Maxine gotten her mugger from? It sounded like a perfectly logical Manhattan assumption. Maybe she was right. But August Frye was in no mood for the happenstance. He had felt somehow cheated by the explanation of Stanley's death, resisting the claim that it had been an accident. And even if there had been some accidental element in Stanley's death, he did not feel that Priscilla Cortez and Hastings were exonerated. They had been in the process of kidnapping Stanley when he was killed. As far as August was concerned, that made them murderers.

Cable had shrugged. "The prosecutor is not interested in metaphysical explanations."

"Metaphysical! This is so concrete you can smell it."

"Take your first assumption, kidnapping. It can't be proved."

"They admit it."

"Now they have a lawyer. Now they say they offered Professor Bledsoe a lift home. Period."

"Do you believe that?"

Cable went into a lengthy spiel about the difference between what he believed to be true, what he by God knew to be true, and what could be established in a court of law playing by rules that tied you into knots.

"Rules I'm in favor of, by the way."

"You don't sound like it."

"The rules are fashioned to prevent innocent people from being guilty. That happens sometimes. I know cases. Nothing's perfect."

"They killed Stanley, James."

"Each man kills the thing he loves."

"Wilde."

"I thought it was Keats."

He was kidding. He'd better be. They would repeal his B.A. if he weren't.

No brandy in his drawer. It might have been his way of mourning Stanley, not drinking in the office. And he would put out that collection of poems, the hell with Larry Gridiron. Old man Bledsoe was eager to pay whatever it cost to immortalize his son. That is what August had promised it would do. Perhaps he would write an interpretative essay, to serve as a preface for the book, *Selected Poems of Stanley Bledsoe*, edited and with an introduction by August Frye. He liked it. He liked everything about it except the need to read through Stanley's output in order to select a dozen or two. The Least Worst Verse of Stanley Bledsoe. A Modern Dunciad.

He pushed back from his desk. There was no reason he couldn't go across the street and have a glass of brandy there.

$\triangledown$

3

F<small>RANCIS</small> <small>CEASCU</small> <small>HAD</small> <small>THE</small> unenviable task of telling Gregory Hackis that Dean Downs was dead. Francis was as tolerant of heterosexual antics as could reasonably be expected, but he could never for the life of him grasp what Gregory saw in Maggie Downs. Maggie. Francis closed his eyes as if to diminish the pain. To think of her as dead did not tax his imagination, since he had never considered her completely real. Some of his friends professed to feel, should one say, "comradeship" with their sisters in oppression, but Francis was not among them. He found women a bore, and he found women like Maggie Downs a bore and a threat. And marveled at the way she controlled Gregory Hackis.

In the presidential office, Hackis sat behind his desk, frowning at something on its surface. The intensity of his expression, the set of his shoulders, inspired confidence in his executive abilities. On the miniature television set before him, the National League playoffs were in progress. Hackis looked up guiltily until he saw it was Francis. Even so, he put the little set away.

"I have bad news, President Hackis." It was his practice to keep everything on the highest level of formality with his employer.

"Strawberry's hamstring?"

118

Francis was seldom nonplussed, but he could not grasp the meaning of what Gregory Hackis had said. He tipped his head to one side and looked receptive.

"Is it something else?"

"Dean Downs has been attacked in the elevator."

The human animal is an amazing entity. Francis watched the phases of Gregory's comprehension of what he had said. Predictably, he leapt to his feet and rounded the desk on the run. He hit the corner of the desk with his upper leg and let out a roar of pain. He limped toward Francis.

"What!"

"Are you hurt?"

Hackis was in obvious pain. Perhaps in an odd way, that helped.

"She was found in the elevator on garage level."

"How is she?"

"Dead."

He got it. He understood it. He leaned over and rubbed his leg, keeping an eye on Francis. "Should I go down there?"

"Should a president go see what has happened to the dean of the college?"

Hackis thought about it. "But I don't want to see her. "

"Then don't. How's your leg?"

"It's killing me."

"Sit down. Who's ahead?"

Within a minute Gregory was back behind his desk, watching the game and rubbing his leg.

"Talk about Strawberry."

Francis had the odd feeling that he did not know the English language, or that Hackis didn't. What on earth was he expected to say about Strawberry?

He slipped out of the office and called Security to get the latest on Maggie. From the office behind him came a sound he at first did not recognize. Then he realized that Gregory Hackis was crying. For Maggie or for his sore leg? No doubt for both. He pulled the door shut.

* * *

The body had been taken away, he was told. His next call was to Wonder Woman, Mrs. Hackis. She would expect him to tell her of this. The voice that answered had a distinctively British accent. It was Thea the Trinidadian maid.

"Mrs. Hackis is not at home."

"This is Francis."

"I realize that. She's not at home."

"Do you know where I could reach her?"

"You might try Healthland on Sixty-sixth."

He took the number from her and dialed it. He was willing to make this one extra step, but if Joyce was not at Healthland he would feel absolved of the responsibility to let her know this news. It was a feature of his interrelations with Wonder Woman that they both knew she knew about Gregory and Maggie Downs but neither of course ever flat out mentioned it. Still, part of the understanding was that he should keep her abreast of the relationship between her husband and Maggie. What he shared with her was what neither would admit was malice. Francis had long thought that Gregory's affair with Maggie could only lead to disaster. The trip to Montego Bay was risky beyond belief. Not that Francis couldn't understand a fling; he himself had frolicked in Haiti when it was still safe. Joyce had known of that trip, and Francis had been waiting for her to move on it. Wonder Woman was deeper or at least trickier than he had thought.

Joyce was not at Healthland.

Francis listened to be certain the sobbing had stopped and then went into the inner office. Gregory stood at the window looking forlornly out at the twilit city. He turned.

"They lost."

The Mets. Dear God. Francis would have preferred to have found him complaining about his sore leg. He felt justified in slipping out.

Phil, the guard downstairs, had come on duty after the ambulance had taken away Maggie Downs's body.

"What happened?" Francis asked, if only to learn what word of mouth had to say.

"Someone jumped her in the elevator."

"Raped her?"

Phil tucked in his chin. "Did you ever try doing it in an elevator?"

"As a matter of fact, yes."

"Maybe you're the man, then. Where were you at the time of the rape?"

The guard's guttural laughter followed Francis into the street. So quickly had poor Maggie's tragedy become the stuff of comedy. Francis shivered and hurried into the darkness.

4

No two versions of a story are ever exactly alike, but seldom are the variations significant. James B. Cable, typing out the account Larry Gridiron was now giving in a somewhat edgy voice, felt that this exercise would establish beyond any doubt that he had shown no favoritism to his old professor. Indeed, he was being harder on him than he would have been on a stranger. Gridiron had missed his dinner and his wife was probably angry at him, but he was their only source of what had actually happened there in the basement garage of Lyndon Johnson.

That Gridiron was no longer flattered by the attention he was getting and was on the verge of blowing up was good. There was more chance of forcing out a memory Gridiron did not know he possessed while the professor was steamed up. Let Gridiron think that suspicion was directed at him. No harm in giving him a little scare. An innocent man would not know what the key facts were and therefore would not hold them back as the guilty would. But nothing essentially new emerged from Gridiron's recorded statement.

On the spur of the moment, he had decided to leave the building by the basement garage and had taken the stairs of the first-floor lobby. Once he got there he balked at the thought of going up the narrow ramp to the street. He hit the elevator button but grew impatient and went back to the stairway. When he got there, he heard the elevator door open and ran back through the parked cars until it was in sight and he saw the door still open.

It was what he had told everyone else, but of course he had reached the point where he was remembering remembering rather than events.

What had to have happened on Gridiron's telling was that Dean Downs, either in the elevator or when the door opened in the basement, was assaulted and killed. Cable preferred its having happened on the way down, there not being much time for strangling the dean before Gridiron got to the elevator. If what Gridiron was telling was the truth.

Cable thought about it. Maggie enters the elevator, somewhere between the seventh floor, where her office was, and the basement. Her assailant enters, assaults her on the way down, and in the basement flees from the elevator, leaving the slumped body of the dean lying half in, half out of the car. Where did he go? Up the ramp, after hiding among the cars? Up the stairway?

Or an already dead Maggie could have been carried onto the elevator and taken to the basement, perhaps to be removed from the premises, when the killer was scared off by the bumbling appearance of Larry Gridiron and fled, leaving his victim's body.

Or . . . Or a dozen other things. Cable dismissed those thoughts. He dismissed Larry Gridiron. He sat turned away from his desk, holding a mug of coffee in both hands as if to slow its cooling, and looked around the precinct room. Fluorescent light sunk in the acoustical ceiling cast an even, dead glow over the desks, the chairs, the files, the paper, paper, paper, in a mimicry of the sun. There was only night now behind the yellowing blinds hanging askew at windows on which gunk prevented much real sun from ever penetrating the room. The ceiling lights were on day and night.

On his way home he stopped at a Blarney Stone and had a Jameson's and water, sipping the whiskey meditatively, trying to disconnect the moment from those that had gone before and those that must come afterward. He particularly did not want to think of home. Home! He would not have thought he would miss Sheila so much. The day she walked out, finally after seven years fulfilling her repeated threat, he had celebrated by going through a six-pack while watching the Giants play. How could he miss such a whining, nagging pain in the neck? But the truth was that he did. Sheila was a bitch, but she had been his bitch. Besides, he was no prize himself.

Where was Sheila now? He assumed in Bayonne with her unmarried sister. There was nothing formal about their breakup, at least as far as he knew; they were separated only physically, not legally. He actually took comfort in that.

The figure moved again. Angled at the bar, half a haunch on the stool, Cable had both the mirror and peripheral vision feeding him images of the bar he sat in. No effort could have turned off instinctive checking out of the place. He turned to the mirror to see who it was that had again changed tables, almost in order to get in his line of vision.

Pregunta! Seeing Pregunta while thinking of Sheila did it. Cable eased himself off the stool, stood, finished his drink, and picked up his cigarette. He quickly put it out. No point in that. Pregunta would already have seen him smoking. Would he put that into his report to Sheila? God, how she would react to that. Willpower, she had told him. That's all it takes. Willpower. Beware someone who has never smoked. Sheila talked as if she had missed out on Original Sin, at least where his faults were concerned. He suggested she quit drinking coffee to show him what willpower was like.

"Coffee and smoking? You think coffee and smoking are the same thing."

That's how the fights began. Did all wives become enemy number one?

Cable left the Blarney Stone, got a cab immediately, and was on his way to Shea before Pregunta could have gotten up from his table. Too bad, in a way. He would like Sheila to know that now if he wanted to go to the goddam ball game, let alone watch the Mets on the tube, he just did it.

The next day he walked past the pustular apprentice in Pregunta's outer office and into the inner sanctum itself. Hunched over Danish and coffee laid out before him on the desk, Pregunta looked up with confusion in his eyes.

"Cable! What the hell . . . "

"Don't talk while you're eating."

At the window, Cable looked down at Lexington. Pregunta had pushed away from his desk and was closing the door to the outer office.

"This is a break, Cable."

"Why are you tailing me?"

"Tailing you!" A gruff bark of a laugh. "I've been trying to run into you."

Blue herringbone jacket, maroon turtleneck, long creased face under the inverted bowl of hair that would have been described in terms of the colors it wasn't, a subspecies of brown. Pregunta was licking Danish from his fingers.

"Who hired you, my wife?"

Pregunta sat down, genuinely surprised. "Is that what you thought?"

"Who, then?"

"Cable, nobody's got me tailing you. That's a fact."

"You're just doing it for practice."

"I wanted to talk to you."

"Your phone been cut off?"

"I couldn't just call you. At least, I don't think I should have. Ethics." Pregunta smiled in mild embarrassment, as if he had just laid claim to heroic virtue. "Anyway, now you're here."

"What's your ethical problem?" By ethics Pregunta meant, first, conduct that kept him out of deep trouble, second, other people's notions of how he ought to behave and, third, irrational restraints on his operation.

"Joyce Hackis is my client."

Cable sat down. "Tell me more."

"I don't have to tell you this, Cable."

"You just want to?"

"Look, if you're not interested in the fact that Mrs. Hackis hired me, say so and get out of here." Pregunta was mad, not least because he had been robbed of the unusual sense of occupying moral high ground. He had sat down again when Cable did, but now made elaborate efforts to rise. Cable lifted a hand.

"Tell me about Joyce Hackis."

"I try to do you a favor and you get on your high horse, busting in here just like a cop."

Pregunta had the usual ambivalence of the private investigator toward the police. His brother had been a cop, but had been killed when his cruiser went out of control chasing a bank robber and wrapped itself around a bridge abutment. His sister worked in Traffic. As private investigators went, there were worse. Cable apologized. He wanted to hear about the president's wife.

"She hired me for the usual reason. Her husband. She was sure he was fooling around. Fooling around! Earl could have handled this one." He meant the kid in the outer office eating junk food from a bag.

"With whom?"

"The dean of the college. Margaret Downs."

Pregunta got out copies of the reports he had sent Mrs. Hackis, and Cable moved his chair closer to the window and looked them over. The usual depressing stuff. Subject followed to apartment of Miss Downs, where he remained for two hours and forty-five minutes. The affair had been regular but not mechanical, by and large at her place, but spiced by out-of-town trips, usually but not always when one or the other had appeared on a meeting's program. Some of the trips were pure hanky-panky, no excuse at all. That was definitely true of the five days in Montego Bay.

"You followed him to all these places?"

"She was paying, and she insisted."

"The last of these is dated last June."

"That's when she decided she had enough."

"I would say she was right about that."

"Only, she hasn't done anything. I'll be frank with you, Cable. It wouldn't hurt me if it became known that she hired me. She's a notch up so far as clients go."

"Maybe she just wanted to know what her husband was up to."

"Uh-uh. This is a woman scorned, Cable. Of course, she didn't want to go on about it to me, but she had to fill me in somewhat. They were childhood sweethearts. She's been with him all the way. She thinks she had as much to do with his being where he is as he did. It was obvious she meant to take him for everything she could."

"Maybe she changed her mind."

"Maybe she did. Maybe she decided on direct action."

Cable waited for Pregunta to say it, almost superstitious about not wanting to be the first to link Joyce Hackis with the death of Maggie Downs.

"You no longer worked for her after this June report?"

"She called me off, saying she had enough. But enough for what? I kept waiting for something to blow up, you know? A headline, a gossip item, something." Pregunta grinned wryly. "I had half a notion to plant a story myself, get the scandal rolling. I figured, at a trial, I'd be called to testify. Not bad for business."

"Maybe she's just slow."

"The Downs killing, Cable. Think about it. As soon as I heard, I thought, that's her solution. Do away with the other woman."

"That's why you've been wanting to talk to me?"

"What's wrong with the idea?"

"I'll let you know."

"We never talked," Pregunta said, following him into the outer office. "You found all this out by yourself."

"How self-effacing you are, Pregunta."

The investigator's eyes slid toward his assistant. "Go to hell, Cable."

He went to the precinct, which was the next best thing.
For half an hour, he read his reports of the questioning of
Priscilla Cortez. He also read the coroner's report on Margaret Downs. Death by strangulation, a smooth heavy cord,
which had not been found. Apparently, it had been looped
over her head from behind. Death had not come easily.

Cable lit a cigarette and tuned out the cacophony of the
room where other cops were interviewing suspects, listening
to complaints, or studying the sports page with the concen-
tration the devout reserve for Holy Writ. Cable let a scene
form in his mind. Maggie Downs enters the elevator, in a
hurry, at day's end. Haddock had said she was on her way
to meet a potential donor at the Union League Club.

"Who?"

"You want his name?"

"If you have it."

He could see Haddock's estimate of him dropping. The
assistant dean had promised to get the name for him. The
question had been diversionary in part, desperate in part.
When you know nothing of what has happened, you cannot
rule out anything as irrelevant.

Priscilla Cortez had never mentioned Joyce Hackis. She
hadn't said much about the president either, practically
begging him not to mention she was Hackis's chauffeur.

Cable picked up the phone and called the garage.

On the way to Brooklyn to see Priscilla Cortez, out on bail
thanks to her lawyer and a bail bondsman, also on leave of
absence from her job, he made his mind a blank slate on
which nothing was written. He kept writing nothing on it
all the way.

"Who's driving him while you're off?" Cable asked her.
Her apartment was bright and feminine, full of plants and
what seemed like half a dozen cats.

"Have you met Francis Ceascu?" She was lisping.

"After you serve your sentence, maybe you'll get your job
back."

"You son of a bitch."

Cable laughed. "You and Roy will get off scot-free, don't worry about it."

"Is that a promise?"

"Tell me about Joyce Hackis."

"I don't know anything about her."

She didn't like the switch. It became clear that she didn't much care for Joyce Hackis, though it was hard to see why. No, she had never been asked to drive the president's wife. That wasn't her job.

"Who said so?"

"Nobody said so. My job is to drive Hackis. Period. I don't have to be told I don't drive other people."

"How about Maggie Downs?"

"Tell me what happened."

"Did you ever drive Maggie Downs?"

She got up and opened a window when he took out his cigarettes. "Do you mind?" he asked.

"I have the feeling it isn't going to matter. Look, I drove whoever Hackis had with him. In that sense I drove his wife, sure. And I drove the dean, too. And lots of other people. If they were with Hackis."

"You drove Maggie Downs when she was with Hackis?"

"Of course."

Cable consulted the list he had made from Pregunta's reports. "Last March third, you drove Hackis and Downs to JFK?"

"What's that list?"

"Trips the dean went on."

"Jesus."

He lit his cigarette. Priscilla leaned forward and rubbed the palms of her hands on the knees of her jeans, looking at Cable with anguish.

"You see what I'm getting at, Priscilla?"

"You think she killed Maggie?"

"Do you?"

"It never once crossed my mind. Look, Downs had enough enemies to make a longer list than the one you've got there.

What do you think Mrs. Hackis had against the dean?"

"I want you to tell me that."

"Not on your life."

"Priscilla, I've got all the facts. The Kansas City trip, the New Orleans trip, the trip to Chicago, Denver twice, the good old mile high city, and of course Montego Bay."

She nodded through the list and, when he was finished, shook her head. "Smart people are dumber than the rest of us, do you know that?"

"I'm too dumb to know."

"Ha-ha. Okay, you know about Hackis and the dean. I didn't tell you. I believe in loyalty."

"He doesn't."

For half a second she thought the remark referred to her, then she got its point. "Yeah."

"Did his wife know?"

"She would have had to try in order not to. I warned him."

"Warned him about what?"

"He seemed to think he was invisible or something. Anybody could see what was going on. Francis knew." She stopped. "He told you, didn't he?"

"No."

"Oh, come on. It had to be Francis."

"It wasn't, but go ahead. Anybody could see what was going on."

"He was flagrant."

"Oh, I don't know. A lot of people were surprised to hear about you and Roy."

"Neither of us is married."

"Even so. An older woman and a student."

She tried unsuccessfully to see this as a description of Roy and herself. "It's not the same thing."

"So you think Mrs. Hackis knew?"

"Let's say I was afraid she'd find out."

"Afraid of what?"

"I didn't know. Now I do." She narrowed her eyes as she said it.

"Maggie Downs was strangled to death. She was not a small woman. You think Mrs. Hackis could do a thing like that?"

"Have you met her?"

"Not yet."

$\triangledown$

5

AUGUST FRYE SAT IN a Franciscan church in a back pew
with his eyes closed, the vestige of incense and wax in the
quiet air an olfactory reminder of long ago. His wife had been
Catholic, and from time to time, say twice a year, he had
accompanied her to Mass, half wishing he shared the faith
of those around him. Those occasions turned his wife into
a stranger, yet he felt a kind of affinity with the other
worshipers. Dear God, if there is a God . . .

He had Masses said for her soul, acting on her belief, not
his own. But of late he was all but overwhelmed by a sense
of obligation to the dead. The recent dead. Poor Stanley
Bledsoe and now Maggie Downs. Natural death was bad
enough, but Stanley and the dean should by all rights still
be alive. Outliving the young induces a sense of guilt, but of
course he already felt guilty about Stanley's going. It wasn't
right that a life should end like that, without definitive
meaning, just stopping. But the case of Maggie Downs was
worse. Murdered.

He formed the word on his lips, and his eyes opened. Far
ahead of him the gaudy altar glittered in the semidarkness,
vigil lamps, the glint of gilt, a light recessed in the ceiling
playing on bronze candlesticks and on the crucifix mounted
over the center of the altar. Someone had put some kind of

rope around Maggie's neck and twisted the life out of her.

August shivered. He sat forward, about to let his knees touch, but caught himself. He actually looked around to see if anyone had witnessed August Frye almost on his knees in church. Gridiron? What would Gridiron say? Larry had lost what little moral clout he had by the way he had taken to departmental administration. Oh, to hell with Larry Gridiron. He glanced toward the sanctuary. Sorry. He had stopped here on his way to the memorial service for Maggie Downs, intending to say a private prayer for her. For ten minutes he had sat here, his head a booming, buzzing confusion, as William James had put it. For someone who supposedly had lived the life of the mind for over four decades, he certainly had trouble putting consecutive thoughts together when he wasn't speaking. It was better just talking to himself, and to whoever else might be listening in.

May she rest in peace. Stanley too.

His mind drifted to himself. How long before it was August Frye who was gone, to be briefly remembered before the waters of forgetfulness closed over him? It seemed unfair that his wife and Stanley and now Maggie had him to remember them. By the time he himself died, there would be no one alive to mourn him.

By the time he left the church and caught a cab to go to the funeral home in the Seventies, August was a bit miffed with the universe and its maker.

The Hackises were in the front row, of course, and Larry and Maxine Gridiron next to them. The cadaverous man in the ill-fitting dark suit turned out to be Maggie's cousin, the sole relative there. But then, this was a university memorial and Maggie's colleagues from Lyndon Johnson were there in force, if not precisely in grief or mourning, then in the grim temporary solidarity that a death in the midst produces. August was late. He nodded at James Cable, who stood against a back wall of the quasi-chapel. After the murky warmth of the Franciscan church, this place was bogus indeed. It had been designed to waffle between religious belief and its absence, between sorrow and matter-of-factness, between hail and farewell. Just when it had struck him that it was odd Cable was here, Hackis rose to speak.

He gripped the podium with both hands and looked out at his colleagues with something approaching terror in his eye. Had the rumors about Hackis and Maggie been true? If they were, he was in an awkward spot, probably wondering how many of those looking back at him knew. It seemed tasteless for him to be giving her eulogy, employer speaking of employee, so to speak, if there had been much more between them. The one eye he seemed determined not to meet was his wife's.

"There are seasons in our life as in the year," Hackis began, and August's groan was audible. Ahead of him, Wilma Trout stirred. It was difficult to tune Hackis out as his analogy got him into complications. He spoke of autumn leaves and winter, and where exactly he thought Maggie was in this scheme of things was impossible to say. Administrators had canned speeches for all occasions, didn't they? Hackis also had Francis Ceascu, who stood to one side of him like an acolyte, a study in resignation. The pain on his thin face could have been produced either by the loss of Maggie Downs or the ineptitude of the president at the podium. August tried without success to make his mind a blank. Failing that, he would have welcomed distraction of the kind that had assailed him in the Franciscan church. But now his attention focused unwaveringly on Hackis.

It was over in twelve minutes—Frye timed it—which only proved the relativity of duration. *A day in thy courts is an eternity.* These words formed in August Frye's mind, arising from who knew what layer of memory. The mourners milled uneasily about, mumbling incoherent phrases, embarrassed. August was happy to get outside again.

"Pretty bad," Cable said.

"It's not the sort of thing you'd want to get good at, speaking over the dead."

"Where are you off to?"

August consulted his watch as if a crammed schedule demanded careful disposition of his time. "I was thinking of asking you to come have a drink."

"Great minds," Cable said.

"Indeed."

Seated in captain's chairs at a compact wooden table in an uptown bar, August wondered if Cable could become the companion Gridiron had somehow ceased to be. Larry always found an excuse to cancel their weekly outing now, and there was little regret in his voice when he mentioned the reason. August permitted himself to doubt that Larry was telling the truth. As chair of the department, truth would have lost its intrinsic value for him; truth and its opposites were merely possible means of exercising power.

"Did you know Hackis and Maggie Downs were carrying on?"

"Carrying on," August mused. "What an evocative phrase, James."

"If true, that would not have contributed to his performance just now."

"Rumors, James, rumors. *De mortuis nil nisi bonum.*"

"Whatever that means, it isn't rumor, it's fact. Mrs. Hackis hired an investigator named Pregunta."

"Well, well."

"I've seen his reports."

August Frye lifted his glass and looked at it. Aristotle contemplating the bust of Marilyn Monroe. "These are reports he made to Joyce Hackis?"

"You got it."

"She knew her husband was carrying on with Maggie?"

Cable nodded. And for the first time he lifted his glass to his mouth. Had conveying this information been the reason for James's coming to the service? The significance of an affair between Hackis and Maggie dawned on August belatedly. Hackis had been unfaithful to his wife. His wife knew it. Now the other woman was dead. Problem solved. August

Frye tried to remember how Joyce Hackis had behaved during the memorial, but he had paid no attention to her. He asked Cable about it.

"Nothing. She sat through it like the rest of you and that was that."

"Have you talked with the Hackises yet?"

"You think I should?"

"She could have done it, James."

"Why?"

"Why! You just told me why. Her suspicions had been aroused, she hired a detective, and she found out it was true. Her husband and Maggie were carrying on. Believe me, Joyce Hackis would not have taken that lying down." He gestured with his hand. "Bad way of putting it."

"She's taller than he is."

"And stronger."

"She could have done it."

"You haven't talked with her yet?"

It was James's turn to look at his watch. "In forty-five minutes."

They had another drink, which took them to the time that Cable had to leave to keep his appointment with Joyce Hackis.

"We're meeting at Healthland."

"Where's that?"

He had it written down. August didn't really care. He waved Cable on his way and, his gesture being interpreted as a reorder, let it ride. It seemed fitting that he get a bit of a buzz on for Maggie. It seemed somehow symmetrical with his dropping by the Franciscan church.

The more he thought of it, the more the Amazonian Mrs. Hackis seemed the explanation of what had happened to Maggie. Love, he mused, explains most acts of violence. Maybe she thought at first she wanted to unload Hackis, get the goods on him and take him for all she could in the divorce settlement. But the Hackises had been together a long time, a very long time considering their age and the Age. Actually, to drop her husband, no matter how attractive it must have seemed when she first learned he was unfaithful to her, would have been difficult, particularly when she realized she was leaving a free road to Maggie.

The wronged wife hates the other woman, not her husband. Joyce's wrath would have been directed at Maggie.

August nodded. It all made sense. Ah, the vagaries of love. Maggie might be out of the way now, but he could imagine that the suspicion Cable felt of Joyce would soon produce the needed evidence. Poor Hackis would end up with neither of his women.

$\triangledown$

6

CAUGHT AND HELD BY her sweatband, Joyce Hackis's hair was wringing wet. Her body-clinging gym attire made it difficult to know just where to let his eyes rest. She seemed to sense Cable's embarrassment and drew a terry-cloth robe over her shoulders. The woman could have made it as a woman wrestler if she wanted. Did she pump iron, too? Cable was glad for the robe. He had been wondering if she could make her muscles ripple on command.

"I've talked with Pregunta," he said.

"You can't smoke here!"

Cable was surprised to find that his package of cigarettes was indeed in his hand. He had not consciously taken them from his pocket. Well, that's what a habit is. He put the cigarettes away.

"He showed me the reports he gave you."

"I thought that was a confidential relationship."

"Only when it doesn't involve concealing matters relevant to a crime."

Her eyes seemed to move over his face in search of the significance of his remark. "Crime?"

"Maggie Downs was murdered. Strangled."

"By a mugger."

"Why do you say that?"

She made a face. "Because mugging threatens to become an Olympic sport in this city. A woman in our building was killed in an elevator just last spring in a very similar way."

"Is that what gave you the idea?"

The terry-cloth robe fell open when she stood up. Cable decided he would not want to tangle with Joyce Hackis. What would it do to a man, being beaten by a woman? Probably not all that much. Males are beaten by women for the first decade of their lives at least. Nonetheless, he kept the table between them.

"When did you first suspect your husband?"

"Suspect him of what?"

The room they were in was maybe twelve by twelve, low ceiling, infested by a jiggly music that crept in through wall speakers.

"Will you tell me where you were last Thursday afternoon when Maggie Downs was found dead?"

"I will not."

Coming to Healthland had been a mistake; he could see that now. This overheated, pastel place with the soothing music oozing from its walls was her turf. She stood there with hands on hips, her body concealed and revealed by the attire that was like an extra layer of skin, the sweatband giving her the look of a noble savage, staring at him with the contempt he was beginning to think he deserved. He knew plenty about the motive her husband had provided her, they had checked out all the trips and found Pregunta's information accurate, but he had no idea what effect such knowledge would have on Joyce Hackis. That she was not your run-of-the-mill wife was more than apparent. He decided not to lose the advantage Pregunta's information gave him.

"No, I didn't think you would. How do I get out of here?"

She seemed half disappointed to see him go. It was now obvious to him that she was enjoying this. If she had indeed done away with Maggie, she would have anticipated being questioned. Even if she had assumed that Pregunta's discovery was simply between her and the investigator, she must have known that her husband's affair with Maggie Downs could not be a complete secret.

"I'll show you."

Walking beside her, Cable felt he was on a beat again in a tough territory, though everyone they saw was in a health-nut uniform, in frenzied pursuit of immortality.

"I *will* answer your question, Mr. Cable. I must have been here in Healthland when that dreadful thing happened to Maggie Downs."

"How often do you come here?"

"Every day." She said it as if she were repeating a resolution. "I love it."

Cable was glad to get out of there. He lit a cigarette before starting the car. Talking to people at Lyndon Johnson about Joyce Hackis was fine, but what could Francis Ceascu and August Frye really know about her? And Priscilla Cortez? He needed to learn a lot more about Joyce Hackis. The woman he had just talked to at Healthland might or might not have killed her husband's girlfriend. That she was physically capable of it was clear enough; that she had a motive in her husband's infidelity was undeniable. What he did not know, what the prosecutor would have to know, was whether or not she was the kind of person to act on that knowledge. And, of course, first of all he had to know if she was indeed at Healthland when Maggie was killed.

Stephanie Schwartz drew that assignment. Cable wasn't going back to Healthland again ever. The place gave him the creeps. It made him want to smoke and drink and eat fatty foods, defy all the odds and outlive the earnest sweating patrons of Healthland and all similar workout places across the country. Politicians spoke of the gap between the rich and the poor. That between the grossly fat and preternatu-rally lean was more obvious. A stroll through any suburban mall could make you believe that every other person in the country was carrying maybe a hundred extra pounds. They sat at little tables eating their choice of pizza, Mexican food, Chinese food, burgers and fries, hot dogs, chicken, malted

milks in a variety of flavors—lethal. An exchange cop from
Greece had pointed to the fatties as evidence that Americans
consumed most of the good things of the earth. Maybe. But
Cable found overeating more humanly understandable than
the fierce asceticism of Healthland.

"Just drop by and ask?" Stephanie Schwartz had a mole
on her cheek and a fetching gap between her front teeth, and
maybe by the turn of the century would be a cop.

"Or you could join up."

"I work out at the Y."

"They offer an introductory lesson at Healthland."

"Are you serious?"

"No. Find out what records they keep and how accurate
they are. Do people sign in or what?" He wrote down Joyce
Hackis's name and the half hour within which Maggie died.
"See if it's beyond doubt that this person was there then."

One of the newsmagazines had done a lot of background
research on the Hackises when he was a congressman and
brought it up to date when he was appointed president of
Lyndon Johnson. Cable was given monitored access to it and
spent an hour in the building on Madison Avenue, taking
notes. He should tell August Frye of the similarities between
being a cop and being a graduate student. Then the checking
out and phone calls began. After three days, he had a far
better sense of Joyce Hackis and her husband.

Joyce Leary had been born in Dalton, Nebraska, the
daughter of a banker, indeed his only child. Her mother died
when Joyce was four years old. A result of this was that she
became inseparable from her father, more of a son than a
daughter to him. Quintin Leary was as dedicated a sports-
man as he was a banker, and Joyce's childhood had been a
Midwest heaven of fishing and boating and hunting in
season. At the age of fourteen, she had flown north with her
father and several of his friends to fish the Alaskan wilder-
ness. It was on that occasion that, wearing hip boots, fishing
her section of the river, she turned to see a bear on the shore

not twenty feet away. She had fed him her catch, fish by fish, lobbing them shoreward to him while she moved slowly downstream until another of the company came into view. Only then did she dare cry out.

This information about her had been collected for a possible cover story on her husband when Gregory Hackis was making a name for himself as the scourge of the banks that had made fortunes on the plight of midwestern farmers. The big banks forgave loans in the billions to banana republics but held American farmers to the last pound of flesh. Unquote. It was the fact that the same banks then turned around and bought up those farm loans that added to the young congressman's outrage. Hackis emoted on the house floor in a series of after-hour speeches carried by C-Span that captured a freakish share of the TV audience because of an NFL players' strike. He had become a kind of underground celebrity. If the players' strike had not been settled, if the cover story had been run, who knew what might have happened to Gregory Hackis's political career? At the next election, a presidential year, he had lost to a new face in the opposite party and called it quits. Eight years later, he became president of Lyndon Johnson.

The irony associated with Hackis's claim for political attention was that Joyce's father had been ruined by an embezzling charge. Gregory had been a very junior figure in the bank at the time Mr. Leary fell. His father-in-law's peculations were page-one stuff in Dalton and made the Omaha and Lincoln papers on an irregular basis. A local scandal, maybe, but Dalton was Joyce Hackis's world. Reading the photocopies of the Dalton *Courier*'s impassioned coverage of the trial, Cable became engrossed in the account of Gregory Hackis's testimony. A defense witness, he had proved to be the prosecution's best weapon. Outside the courtroom, he broke down. Joyce Hackis was there at her husband's side. "My father is innocent. He will be proved innocent by the rules he taught me." He was found guilty. Before sentencing, he confessed and spurned leniency. He quoted his daughter. There was only one moral and legal code, and he stood condemned by it. Apparently, he thought the punishment insufficient. Within a month of his arrival at Leavenworth, he committed suicide in his cell.

Cable sat back, realized he was smoking a cigarette, and thought of that drama on the plains nearly twenty years ago. Almost Grecian in its starkness. He would never have suspected this background for the Amazonian bodybuilder and the smooth self-serving president of Lyndon Johnson. Those congressional speeches seemed a continuation of the pursuit of rectitude. Had Gregory and Joyce lost that almost biblical sense of retribution for wrong they had learned from her father? What had happened to Maggie Downs in the elevator at Lyndon Johnson did not seem remote from the Hackises who had emerged from his research.

Blowing smoke at the ceiling, Cable imagined Joyce in gym clothes strangling the life out of Maggie Downs after surprising her in the elevator. Afterward, she could have jogged right out of the basement garage and down the street. That was compatible with Stephanie's report that Joyce Hackis had signed in at Healthland an hour before the time of Maggie's death. The center had no record as to how precisely she had spent the time or indeed if she had spent it on the premises. And Joyce Hackis was a jogger, doing ten miles on alternate days on the streets of Manhattan.

And then Stella Houston came to see him.

7

Stella Houston would have found it easier to despise the males of the race if women were not so incredibly stupid. Oh, she knew this could be more than adequately explained as the consequence of centuries of oppression. The enemy was within, bred in the bone, washed into the brain from infancy, probably before, the womb that enveloped the girl child transmitting its own subservient code to her. Submit, obey, carry, nurse, slave, obey. That was the female treadmill that had been developed over the centuries so that women ended by accepting it as if it were their very nature. There were Jews who had sought to ingratiate themselves with their Nazi oppressors; the slave can come to love his servitude; there are even Irish Anglophiles. There were women who loved being women, and Maggie Downs, despite her success in a man's world, was one of them.

This was all the more disappointing to Stella because Maggie possessed the proletarian credentials that she herself lacked. Stella had gone from Bennington through Barnard to Oxford, becoming progressively more radical as she went. She had cut sugarcane in Cuba, spent a week in Managua; her days were filled with protests, her life a prolonged defiant cry against the way things are. But it troubled her that she was open to the charge of radical chic. She might wear shapeless skirts and serviceable shoes and generally cultivate an unkempt air, but this did not alter the fact that she had inherited a massive amount of money, first from her father and then from two distant relatives who had outlived all their other heirs. On her last visit to Boston, Stella had been given the figure stating her current worth. "Not quite four million," Winthrop had said, sliding the paper across the desk to her. He spoke as if he were sucking lemon drops. Stella quickly put the report into a bag emblazoned with the Sandinista emblem. She longed to be poor and exploited, but it never entered her mind to get rid of her money. Nor was she a contributor to the causes she espoused, too ashamed to let it be known how wealthy she was. She told herself that being a woman was all the oppression she needed.

Maggie Downs, by contrast, had come up through the ranks, transcending poverty and an all but illiterate Catholic family—she had actually done her undergraduate work at Marymount—her extraordinary GREs plucking her from mediocrity. She went to Columbia, where she lost her faith and got her Ph.D. It was difficult to say what Maggie knew, in any serious sense of the term, but she had for Stella Houston all the authority of a woman of the people. In the presence of the dean, Stella felt an awe induced in her by gun-toting female warriors in Nicaragua. It was evident that Maggie had her sights set much higher than the deanship.

When Stella first heard that Maggie had become the mistress of the ineffable Hackis, she literally clamped her hands over her ears. No believer had ever been more appalled by a blasphemous remark. She glared at Ginsberg.

"What a filthy thing to say." Her words echoed in her head. She removed her hands from her ears.

But others in the lounge came to his defense. "Grow up, Stella," Ginsberg said smugly. "Every step up the ladder has been a horizontal move by Maggie. Do I make myself clear?"

Wilma Trout had the decency to say that the others could not possibly know such a thing for sure.

"Only his driver knows for sure," said Ginsberg. Stella

had never before noticed Ginsberg's tendency to smirk.

The driver referred to was Priscilla Cortez, who chauffeured the presidential limousine. No uniform could have concealed the feisty iconoclast Priscilla was. Stella felt an immediate affinity with the woman. Alas, it was not reciprocated. Priscilla reacted with wariness to Stella's overtures, responding monosyllabically, never free for a cup of coffee. This was Stella's cross, to feel sisterhood and solidarity with those who held her at arm's length as a member of the oppressing classes.

"I spent a week in Managua," she said to Priscilla.

"Hawaii?"

Stella repressed the urge to correct. "How long have you been driving?"

"Since I was sixteen."

Stella would guess the girl to be thirty, maybe older. "Can you get a chauffeur's license at that age?"

Priscilla looked at her as if she were retarded, and indeed Stella's sense of lamentable superiority deserted her as she moved into the unfamiliar territory that was daily life for the masses. Priscilla meant that she had begun stealing cars at sixteen.

"Joyriding. It was a big thing in my block in Brooklyn. Not that we stole cars there. Nobody in our block owned a car."

"Is Cortez Spanish?"

"Puerto Rican."

"*Puedo hablar español un poco.*"

Priscilla ignored this phrase-book effort. She obviously wanted to get back to the guard shack where she wasted her time between drives. Hers had to be the least demanding job in the city, yet she clearly gloried in it. Her dream was to own her own stretch limousine and sign up with one of the rental agencies. Why, she might drive celebrities. She'd heard stories. Rock stars behind the tinted glass, snorting coke, even mating—Priscilla used the Anglo-Saxon, a word Stella would never get used to because, she told herself, it enshrined the notion of male dominance—as they were

driven from LaGuardia to their hotel. Big shots from foreign
lands wanting to move anonymously through Manhattan to
their country's embassy.

Priscilla's seemed a modest enough ambition. How easily
Stella might have made the girl's dream come true and given
her the money for the limousine. She knew better. The one
lesson she had accepted from her father was that nothing
creates enemies more surely than generosity. "We never
forgive those who have helped us," he said. Of all the
apodictic remarks he had made to her, that one alone
survived the years. There was a particular danger of being
misunderstood in offering money to a younger woman.

Stella wanted to be loved for herself alone. Had she ever
been? Has anyone? Her sexual orientation, while apparently
no secret, was not for all that a public matter. She had never
come out, despite the urging of well-meaning friends. A
residual homophobia? Most likely. Again, the enemy within,
that repressive code so deeply ingrained that it sounded like
her very nature speaking.

A Christmas gift after months of just saying hello broke
the ice, and at last Priscilla felt comfortable with her. It was
nearly all destroyed when Stella said offhandedly, lying, that
her frequent flyer plan had provided her with two free tickets
to the Carribean. Did Priscilla want to go?

"Free?"

"The more you fly, the more free miles you earn. Sooner
or later, it adds up to something interesting."

"Two of them?"

"That's right."

"I'll take them."

Not exactly what Stella had had in mind, but what could
she do? Priscilla obviously had another companion in mind.
When Stella found out who it was, she went through a
wrenching three days fighting racism in her heart with every
ounce of moral energy she possessed. But nothing she could
summon diminished her deep irrational hatred of Roy
Hastings.

Disastrous as the trip suggestion turned out, it also provided the occasion for Priscilla's telling Stella about Gregory Hackis and Maggie Downs.

"They went to Montego Bay," Priscilla said. "Maybe Roy and I will too."

"They took a trip to Jamaica together?"

"Isn't that where Montego Bay is?"

It was not difficult to find the approximate date of this trip, although Francis Ceascu was less cooperative at first.

"Stella, why should you care?"

He wondered if she was jealous. Was she? Stella honestly did not think so. She felt at too much of a disadvantage with Maggie for anything to develop, if anything was in the cards, which she doubted. Maggie was ferociously heterosexual. But Gregory Hackis? It was incredible that Maggie should think so little of herself.

"Is it true?" she asked Francis.

Once begun, he bared his soul, of course, and what a story it was. Francis saw it as stupidly risky for the president, and there was something to that.

"Does his wife know?"

"Sweetheart, if she doesn't, she is dumber than we think."

Stella did not think Joyce Hackis was dumb at all. And Maggie was smart. Why are women so incredibly stupid where men are concerned?

"It's a two-way street, Stella," Francis said.

No doubt. Nonetheless, it was depressing. Maggie, Joyce, Priscilla. Stella had never felt so isolated. Over coffee with Priscilla she spoke her mind on the stupidity of the dean.

"You sound like Roy."

"That's hard to believe."

Priscilla laughed like a man, throwing back her head and letting go. "You know what I mean. He hates that woman."

"Why?"

"It's a long story."

A disgruntled student. God save us, Stella Houston thought. What teacher at Lyndon Johnson was unaware of the fact that a good percentage of the students thought they had a constitutional right to passing grades and a degree? There was an implicit threat in this attitude, of course. Stella preferred to think that it all stemmed from the dissolution of bourgeois society. This made giving high grades seem a blow struck for radical change.

Then young Bledsoe was gone and August Frye's fear that dirty work was afoot proved well founded. Stella nearly passed out when August told the story in the lounge. Priscilla and Roy?

And now Maggie too was dead. Strangled. Overpowered in the elevator by an obviously powerful person. When Priscilla was released, Stella found it difficult to talk with her. At any moment, she was sure, Roy Hastings would be arrested.

But nothing happened. No one made the connection between his reasons for harassing Bledsoe and his hatred of the dean. It occurred to her that no one knew. She herself knew only because Priscilla had confided in her. That made it a delicate matter, of course. Until she convinced herself that this was a chance for Priscilla to free herself from her unhealthy passion for Roy Hastings.

So Stella went to talk to James Branch Cable.

8

IF NOTHING ELSE IT had symmetry, Cable suggested, and Stella Houston agreed. Two deaths, one accidental, one murder, same killer.

"He's an animal," Stella said.

"We all are."

"Let's not get into that."

"I meant all humans. Rational animals."

"Hmph."

"Just about anyone might have killed Dean Downs."

"Lieutenant Cable, that is ridiculous and you know it. Maggie Downs was not a weak woman, and I doubt very much if she went quietly into that dark night. Her assailant had to be large and strong."

"There are lots of large and strong people who could have done it. You, for instance."

Her smile suggested that she had just removed him from the category of rational animals. "Was Maggie Downs robbed? No. Was Maggie Downs raped? No. Are there any other impersonal motives, ones that might have prompted a stranger to strangle her in that elevator? I know of none. Her killer was someone who knew her and who had reason to hate her."

"Someone like Roy Hastings."

"Not like. The man himself. He had embarked on an absurd campaign to have a grade Bledsoe gave him last spring changed from failure to pass. Gridiron had caved in. Maggie Downs refused to make the change. He has been lurking outside her office of late. She mentioned it to me. More amused than afraid. She would have been better advised to be afraid."

"Gridiron agreed to change the grade?"

"In the most craven manner. It is one thing to have illiterates representing the higher institutions of the nation on the sporting fields. It is quite another to pretend that the unteachable have learned something."

"Did you ever have Roy Hastings in class?"

"Hardly. Jane Austen is not his cup of tea."

"It would help if someone could put Roy Hastings in the vicinity of the basement garage at the time Maggie was attacked."

"Lieutenant, I've told you. He's been hanging around her office."

"On that day?"

"Talk with Haddock, Maggie's associate dean. If anyone saw him, it would be Haddock."

Stella Houston was a fruitcake, sitting there like a peasant, knees spread under the full skirt, leaning toward him, an expression of contemptuous condescension on her face. She did all she could to exclude males from her classes. Her course titles all involved feminism in some way, the better to accomplish this aim. Feminism in Jane Austen was not farfetched. Nor was Feminism in George Eliot and Hardy. But tracing the spoor of raised female consciousness in *The Old Curiosity Shop* and *Ayala's Angel* took more ingenuity. Feminism in *Little Women* was a recurrent offering, very popular. That she should come to him and accuse Roy Hastings of killing Maggie Downs was nutty. He knew that. But he also knew he was fascinated by the suggestion. Fascinated enough to broach it to August Frye.

"Uh-uh," he said, shaking his head without even giving the idea a moment's thought. "Bledsoe, yes. I could see him killing poor Stanley. But not Maggie. The motive is the obvious one. Love. Love betrayed. Hell hath no fury . . . "

They were having dinner in a bar and grill on Thirty-fourth Street, more bar than grill, but the steaks were good. So were the drinks. Cable realized that he could acquire a taste for manhattans. Frye certainly had. He was already on his second.

"Don't try to keep up with me, James."

"Don't worry. This is more or less official."

"If you take seriously every harebrained guess of the faculty, you will never get any time off. What basis did Stella have for such an accusation?"

He told her about the grade change. "Apparently, Gridiron agreed but Maggie Downs said no."

"Larry said yes!"

"So she claims."

"How could she know if he had? It's not something he would announce or even admit to. James, a wager. Ask Larry Gridiron if he had agreed to change a grade posthumously and he will deny it."

"You think he didn't do it?"

"I didn't say that."

After attending to his steak for a minute, Cable said, "You and Gridiron are pretty good friends, aren't you?"

"As close as brothers." Frye sipped his manhattan. "Cain and Abel."

"What happened?"

"Larry sold out. He became chair of the department." The words were strong, but August Frye's voice was gentle. "That is how Larry would describe it, anyway. The poor man is weighed down with guilt and self-loathing. It is hard to see why. He was chair once before, long ago. Some chairmen go to heaven. Not many, but some. Even Faust could have been saved."

"The coach?"

"That's not funny. Did you know Max Brand's real name was Faust?"

"I didn't know Max Brand was a phony name."

August Frye shook his head. "To think you were within a whisker of a doctorate."

"A close shave."

With eyes closed in pain, August signaled for another drink. "I think you should have another too."

"So do I."

And he did. Which is why he arrived at Gridiron's apartment in a less than lucid condition. He and August had agreed to disagree as to what the ultimate explanation for Maggie's death would be. Frye, in a romantic mood brought on by bourbon and sweet vermouth, held out for love and jealousy.

"A classic motif with the roles of Othello and Desdemona reversed."

"You're mixing up the cast. Priscilla and Roy Hastings are Desdemona and Othello."

Frye ignored this even if he heard it. He was too absorbed in his own tale of the strangling of Maggie Downs by Joyce Hackis. When James got his attention, he told August of Joyce's jogging, of the possibility that, having checked into Healthland, she had hit the street running, come by Lyndon Johnson, waylaid Maggie in the elevator, and then gone on her way again.

"So you're coming around to my theory?" August crowed. "Let me have one of those."

He was reaching for Cable's cigarettes.

"Better not. You'll get hooked again."

"Who cares?"

But Cable noticed that Frye did not inhale. Even so, it was dumb of him to take the risk. Celebrating his conviction that Maggie had died for reasons that, if they did not exonerate her killer, were massively extenuating in August's eyes. For all the attractions of the theory, Cable preferred to hold out for something less obvious, something more complicated. The next time he was sober, he meant to ask himself what that might be.

When he asked Larry Gridiron about Hastings's request for a posthumous change of grades, the chairperson of English admitted that such a request had been made.

"And granted. At least by me."

"August Frye said you would deny that."

Gridiron grimaced. "Have you just come from him? I thought you seemed a little drunk. Keep away from him, James, he's a bad influence."

"I owe him a lot. If it weren't for him, I might have ended up a professor."

Gridiron nodded. "You're right. Lyndon Johnson is the bottom of the ladder, but it used to be better, a lot better. Now we have students like Roy Hastings. I'll tell you something, James. I doubt that he can even read."

"Did you really say you were willing to get his grade changed?"

In the other room, Mrs. Gridiron was watching television, the news. Bad as it was, the bad news that got onto television was only a fraction of what any cop was aware of. Gridiron and Frye lamented a decline in the quality of college education, but Roy Hastings represented a deeper problem. Did Gridiron know what the schools out of which Hastings came were like, schools where physical survival was almost an accomplishment?

"It was cowardly of me, I know that. But what can it possibly mean? He actually thinks that grades rather than learning anything are the point of being here. The letter B applied to anything Roy Hastings might do with his mind is meaningless."

"Could he graduate?"

"God forbid."

Roy Hastings had become a more interesting man than when Cable arrested him for importuning Bledsoe. There was something oddly noble in the thought of that big inarticulate product of God knows what background becoming obsessed with the idea of a college education. How had he ever been admitted to Lyndon Johnson? Gridiron must be right. Things were not what they had been. Open admission. Every citizen has a right to a college education. Hastings just took the thought to its next step. He had the right to get passing grades in all his courses.

"What's he really like?" he asked Priscilla Cortez later.

"Roy Hastings? He's a son of a bitch, that's what."

"Hey. I thought you were friends."

"So did I. That's what I get for demeaning myself."

"You don't mean that."

A tortured look, eyes darting about. Her lower lip began to tremble. "He's married!"

She had thought she was doing Roy a favor, no doubt about that. But, in any couple, either the man or the woman assumes that. Cable had not thought he believed this, but then, he had never formulated the thought so clearly before. He had been cast as the inferior in his relationship with Sheila. Maybe he was. Would she have been half as affected by him leaving her as he was by her leaving him? The answer was no. That was her advantage.

"Stella Houston says Roy had been harassing Maggie Downs."

"Stella Houston is a bull dyke."

"But is she telling the truth?"

"Roy thought he passed Bledsoe's course last spring. You already know that."

"You back driving for Hackis?"

"I'm on duty. He's not going many places lately. I take him to his office and take him home again."

"What do you do all day?"

"Answer dumb questions from cops." She took off her sunglasses.

"What happened to your eye?"

She put the glasses on again, quickly. "Nothing."

"Who hit you?"

But she was through answering his dumb questions. He hardly blamed her. It must have been quite an occasion when she found out that Roy was married and had three kids. He shook a cigarette free and extended the pack to her. She looked at it, then at him, then took it. She leaned forward so he could light it.

"You married?" she asked.

"In a way. What is this, a proposition?"

You would have said she was a tough bitch, and she was, but suddenly Cable saw a puzzled little girl who had survived into an adult world and didn't really know what was going on. But she managed a crooked smile.

"I'd rather take cold showers."

"You could take up jogging." He nodded at the Amazonian figure across the street, shoulders close to the body, knees coming up high, the headband keeping the hair out of her eyes.

"Like a clock," Priscilla said, glancing at the clock in the guard shack. "On time, not route. Sometimes she cuts through buildings."

"Yeah?"

"You're sitting here and all of a sudden, swoosh, she goes by." The clock read five-fifteen. "This is her regular time?"

"I don't know about weekends."

"Did you see her the day Maggie Downs was killed?"

The answer was there before Priscilla spoke. Off came the glasses, and she got her feet off the desk.

"Sure I did! She came out of the building." Priscilla looked at the lighted cigarette in her hand, then put it out angrily. "She was here, Cable!"

If she had volunteered it, Cable would have suspected she was just trying to give Joyce Hackis trouble. But the memory had come as memories do, unexpectedly, needing only the right occasion.

"What do you think?" Priscilla asked, eager now. She understood the significance of what she had remembered.

"I think you ought to have that black eye taken care of."

"Get out of here."

And he did. He wanted to see what Stephanie had come up with. Then he would have a serious talk with Mrs. Joyce Hackis.

PART FOUR

▽

What's in a Name?

△

1

THE WINDOWS OF HIS classroom had steel mesh embedded in the glass, making the outside world look like a completed jigsaw puzzle.

"Life is not a jigsaw puzzle," August Frye intoned. "We are not here to put together ready-made pieces. We make the pieces and the design. This is Thornton Wilder's point."

He had come to class unprepared, but at this state of his career that meant little. The vast repertoire of previous courses provided pieces he could put together with infinite variety. Experience had taught him always to use the full names of authors lest Thornton become Billy, Hemingway become Mariel, George or T.S. become Ness. This was not foolproof. He had been asked for the last name of Henry James.

"How many have read the book?"

Two hands went up. Frye didn't believe them. Teaching had become a soliloquy. Something had happened between the time he was young and now. The sullen faces before him listened warily if at all. There had been a period during which he had tried to speak a kind of Esperanto in order to connect with them, but it was the concepts they lacked, not the words. This realization was profoundly depressing. The teacher, he had been told, begins where the student is. But where were his students? He no longer thought he knew.

159

Yet August Frye had no desire to retire, not because he enjoyed teaching, but because he really had no alternative. Even this mute, uncomprehending audience was better than none, and if he spoke only to himself it was pleasant to think that someone was eavesdropping on what he said.

"We knew more in grade school than our graduates do," Gridiron had said.

A sobering thought when one considered the billions spent on education. Gridiron, in the full grips of administrative pessimism now, wondered if the whole experiment in public education had not failed.

"The computer rooms are full," August teased.

Gridiron had a Luddite's hatred of the computer. He also feared it. He had no idea how it worked.

"Word processing," he groaned. "As if words were cheese."

Under Bledsoe's tutelage, August had learned to use a computer. He had made copies of the disks on which young Bledsoe stored his poems, and almost daily sent another batch off to some little magazine, continuing Bledsoe's practice. Even so, there were many that had never been submitted. Perhaps Stanley was a better critic than poet and recognized the quality of his verse. Sometimes there were interesting images.

> Oil and water mix in the rainy street.
> Unpalatable colors glisten there.
> Pumped crude from deep beneath our feet
> Refined oil shines in headlights' glare.

He thought of Bledsoe mesmerized by an oil leak as he prowled the city, his poetic antennae responding with painful sensitivity to the billion stimuli around him. More likely he had been mimicking something he read.

"The fault is not our students but ourselves," he told Gridiron. "We're too damned bookish. Everything comes filtered through novels and plays and poems and ideas. These kids see the raw world and we don't."

"Thank God."

His theory was a bunch of crap, of course. The truth was that one lost touch with the models students were imitating. Even plagiarizing. Bledsoe had been death on plagiarism, and he knew the rock lyrics that were turned in as original work. How cruel that Bledsoe had been accused of plagiarism. His poetry might be derivative and imitative, but he had not consciously stolen from others. Perhaps he should have, although the Henry VIII experience told against it.

After class Frye had lunch with Haddock across the street at Cassidy's where the Reubens were large, greasy, and gaseous.

"How's the acting dean?"

Haddock growled. How old was Haddock? He had gone through the Coast Guard Academy, served twenty years, worked on an M.A. in academic administration, and received it and his discharge at the same time. He had been at Lyndon Johnson ever since.

"How long you been here, Haddock?"

He looked at his watch. "This is my seventh year."

"Is it true Roy Hastings was bothering Maggie?"

"Bothering her? Nothing bothered Maggie. He was hanging around."

"You don't think he killed Maggie?"

Haddock's lashes were very blond although his hair was almost umber. His eyes were never completely open, and when he looked at August his lashes seemed to get in the way.

"I don't know."

"He could have."

"I suppose."

Frye felt a kind of obligation to carry on the conversation, although the noise level at Cassidy's at noon was such that you had to be a lip reader to communicate. Haddock huddled over the table when he told him about Joyce Hackis hiring the detective.

"Jealousy," he said. He had to repeat it in a shout, and

the noise level dipped when he did and several people turned and looked at him.

Haddock shrugged. Frye doubted that Haddock would be the one with whom to develop his thoughts on the Joyce Hackis matter. The acting dean did not have the soul for creative gossip. How could he imagine a woman driven by the sense of rejection to kill the woman who had stolen her husband from her?

Frye went down to Healthland after lunch to sign up for an introductory session, but the woman with the muscular body and ropy hair who sat behind the desk looked at him as she might a used car.

"You'll need a physician's okay."

"I just want to exercise."

She shook her head. "You have to take a physical first. Our insurance requires it."

So much for the thought that he would meet Joyce among exercise machines and worm from her the story of her threatened marriage.

"Could I look around?"

Her expression became suspicious. He opened his coat and she jumped back. The tweedy revelation of his professorial self did not entirely reassure her.

"Joyce Hackis is a friend of mine."

"She's here."

"I thought she might be."

Minutes later, a sweaty Joyce Hackis was showing him around. Frye thought of the baths of Caracalla on whose mosaic floors the feet of long-dead imperialists had trod. He doubted that anyone two thousand years from now would be marveling at the ruins of Healthland.

"She said I need a physical in order to join."

"Oh, it's wise, August. I have twice yearly checkups. You'd be surprised how many people die taking care of themselves."

It was not a punch line, so he only smiled. "Is Gregory a member?"

"A lot of good it does him. He never uses the place."

"Well, he's busy. Is there anyplace we could have coffee?"

She would have been less shocked if he had exposed himself. She led him to a windowless room with pastel walls where various kinds of fruit juice were available from a machine with a voracious appetite for quarters.

He told her the story of Priscilla and Roy, anonymously at first, and she followed with sort of sympathy. But when he told Joyce she knew the woman, her interest quickened.

"Who is it?"

"Your husband's driver."

"Priss, the screwy driver! That's what we call her, August. I can't imagine her with a man young or old, black or white."

"Well, she lost him. Imagine losing the man you love."

Joyce's eyes drifted to the wall, which was the color of the juice she drank.

"I know about Gregory, Joyce."

Her eyes widened as she stared at him. Her free hand enclosed his. And then she was weeping uncontrollably.

2

J AMES CABLE MORE OR less enjoyed being back in touch with August Frye and Larry Gridiron. It connected him with a past he had tried to forget but now realized he never could. And it helped in the Bledsoe and Downs deaths to have people like his old professors to rely on for information. But Frye was becoming a slight pain in the ass. That a professor should sit behind his desk or in a bar and dream up explanations of how two of his colleagues had died was one thing, but Frye was butting in far beyond Cable's capacity for tolerance. No matter who he talked to, it seemed Frye had been there before him. Now, having talked with Stephanie, who had checked out Healthland, Cable went to the exercise club and found a red-eyed Joyce Hackis deep in conversation with August Frye.

"James," August said with an indecisive smile. "How did you know I was here?"

"I didn't. Mrs. Hackis, I'd like to talk with you."

"I am talking already." She squeezed Frye's hand.

"The professor and I are very old friends."

"James is an alumnus," Frye explained.

A bad beginning, and it got worse when Frye said that he and Joyce had been discussing the Pregunta investigation. It galled Cable more because Frye knew of Pregunta only because he had told him. Why couldn't he keep his mouth shut?

"Mrs. Hackis, I am here in an official capacity. There are things I want to ask you. I don't know if you want Professor Frye present, but you might want to consult your lawyer."

"My lawyer!"

"Did you talk to a lawyer after you got Pregunta's reports?" Frye asked her.

"Why on earth would I do that?"

"Mrs. Hackis, please. Given what those reports told you, you must have thought of divorce."

"Not on your life. Even if those reports were true . . ."

"Oh, they were true," Cable said. "We made an independent check."

"Why would you be checking up on my husband?"

"To make certain he had provided you with a motive to kill Dean Downs."

"That's silly."

"Is it? You were seen emerging from the building at about the time Downs died. In your jogging costume."

"I jog almost every day, and that's my customary route. Of course I was seen near the building."

"Earlier, you told me you were at Healthland at the time of the murder. That's more false than true, isn't it? The fact that you jogged the same way every day is neither here nor there, Mrs. Hackis."

"You sound as if you're arresting me."

"That's why I'm here."

"You're serious."

"Yes, ma'am."

She looked at Frye, then back at Cable. "I think I *will* call my lawyer."

She waited as if she expected one of them to object. But Frye pushed the phone toward her. "Do that, Joyce. And don't worry. Your friends will stay with you."

"Do you really think I killed Maggie?"

"My dear, no jury in the world will convict you."

"Jury? My God." She clutched the phone, squeezing her eyes shut. "I don't know the number."

"Call Gregory," Arthur Frye said. "He will know."

Gregory Hackis pulled up in front of Healthland within fifteen minutes of the phone call and came inside with an agitated expression, open coat flapping around him, his complexion almost the color of his red hair.

"What in hell is going on?" he demanded of Cable.

"I'm being arrested," Joyce said in a small voice.

Cable was not annoyed when August Frye explained the situation to him.

"Pregunta? Who's Pregunta?"

"The detective Joyce hired. It's how she knew for sure about you and Maggie Downs."

Hackis actually slid to the floor, not so much in a fainting fall as in the manner of a deflating balloon. August tried to arrest his descent, and was pulled down with the slumping president. From her seat at the desk, Joyce Hackis looked at the two men on the floor as if it were the most ordinary thing in the world for them to be lying there. Cable had noted her credibly incredulous reaction to the charge that she had killed Maggie Downs.

"You hired a detective to follow me?" Gregory asked this of Joyce in wondering tones.

"Don't you dare act shocked! I hired him because I already knew you were up to something, but I had no proof."

"I can't believe you'd be so sneaky, Joyce."

"Me sneaky? You're the one who went off to Jamaica with that woman. Business trip!" She made an exploding sound as she spat forth air.

Had Hackis thought he had deceived his wife so well that she would never learn? Of course he had.

Cable said, "Your wife is going to need a lawyer."

"You're not divorcing me," Hackis yelped. "You can't do that."

"She needs a lawyer because I am arresting her under suspicion of causing the death of Maggie Downs."

Hackis had gotten to one knee now. He looked at his wife, and Cable was glad to see that Hackis did not find it incredible that Joyce would kill Maggie Downs.

Outside Healthland, Hackis insisted that he wanted to take his wife to their lawyer before anything further was done.

"Why not?" August Frye asked. "Where can they run to?"

"Jamaica?"

Hackis's groan was interrupted by a large man with a face like a fist who thrust an envelope into his hand.

"Subpoena," he said.

"What?"

"From the grand jury."

The president of Lyndon Johnson Community College was being hailed before the grand jury to answer questions about the administration of the college.

Priscilla Cortez had come forward as if to protect her employer from the server of the subpoena. Hackis showed no signs of crumbling now. It was Mrs. Hackis who cried out, bringing her hand to her mouth.

"Greg, it's my fault. I gave that detective's reports to the city attorney."

Priscilla helped Hackis to his car.

"I'll go with you," Mrs. Hackis said.

Cable, feeling like an idiot, needed to find out more about the grand jury's investigation before arresting Joyce Hackis. He left the rest of them there and headed for his car. Downtown he learned that Gregory Hackis's conduct of the office of the president of Lyndon Johnson with particular reference to the diversion of official funds for personal benefit in the form of vacations, etc., was under investigation.

$\triangledown$

3

AFTER THE HACKISES WERE driven away in their official automobile, August Frye turned to say something to James Cable and found he was not there. Frye felt as he had as a boy when the others ditched him. In that mood he felt no inclination to walk, although it was a lovely fall afternoon. He hailed a cab, got caught in a traffic jam, and watched the meter record the extent of his folly until he could bear it no longer. He paid, threaded his way through the other stalled cars, and walked to Cassidy's, where he found Haddock with his elbows on the bar gazing at television.

"The grand jury is investigating Hackis," August said, sliding onto a stool and beckoning the bartender. "Want another of those?"

"Grand jury?"

"That's right."

"I will have another. Tell me about it."

"That's all I know."

"What are they looking into?"

Frye wished he hadn't mentioned it. Haddock thought he was being cute, not telling what he knew. But then he remembered Joyce saying she had sent Pregunta's reports to the prosecutor's office. Haddock, having taken all this in, shook his head.

"Those two deserve each other."

"Why would a grand jury care if Hackis had been fooling around with Maggie?"

"Who paid for the trips they took together?"

August looked wise. "Aha."

"Think of the publicity," Haddock mused. "President uses college funds to take sweetheart to Caribbean."

"He'll never live it down."

"Maybe that's what she had in mind."

Frye sipped his drink. What if Haddock were right? Hell hath no fury . . . Had Joyce preferred ruining Gregory to divorcing him?

"Cable was about to arrest Mrs. Hackis on suspicion of killing Maggie."

"On what basis?"

"She was seen coming out of the college building, in her jogging costume, at the time. Gridiron saw no one in the basement, but she could have gone up the stairs and left by the door, which is when she was seen."

Haddock finished the drink Frye had bought him and signaled the bartender. Were the pressures of office getting to the usually moderate acting dean?

"Did you see Mrs. Hackis that afternoon, Haddock?"

"Me?"

"You might have seen her before you went down to the garage with the guard."

"Who did see her?"

"Hackis's driver."

Haddock rolled out his lower lip and rocked his head from side to side. "And Joyce Hackis knew he had been playing around. What do you mean, Cable was about to arrest her?"

"That's when Hackis was served with the subpoena."

"She could have done it," Haddock said. "I saw her in the upper lobby." He narrowed his eyes in search of the memory. "She might have come up the basement stairs. I never thought of it. Gridiron sounded the alarm then, and I went down with the guard."

"You should tell Cable that."

"Maybe he won't arrest her."

"If he's got two people who can place her where Maggie was killed, why wouldn't he arrest her? With the motive she had. God knows she's big enough to have strangled Maggie."

"I'm not volunteering anything. He asks me, I'll tell him."

"Maybe I'll tell Cable what you told me."

Haddock shrugged. Frye took it for permission. First chance he had, he'd bring it up. He asked Haddock if he had known about Maggie and Hackis.

"Monkey see, monkey no tell."

"Meaning you did?"

"Meaning I didn't care one way or the other. Francis Ceascu asked me about it once, did I know. Maybe that made me curious for a time. But why should I care?"

"I never suspected."

"Why should you?"

"It makes me wonder if I know anything about people at all. Think of the last month around here. Stanley Bledsoe gone." The drinks Haddock had ordered arrived. "The mysteries of the human heart."

"Gridiron told me about what you did."

"What do you mean?"

"About the poem you sent in."

August Frye was filled with sudden anger that Larry should mention that now, after what had happened to Stanley.

"Then Maggie," Haddock went on, continuing his thought, "and now I find I am surrounded by hanky-panky. The president disporting himself with the dean, the president's wife hiring a private detective."

"And Larry Gridiron up to God knows what." August was still seething.

"Larry? What's he done?"

"He was willing to change the grade Stanley Bledsoe gave Roy Hastings last spring."

"It can't be done."

"Lucky for Larry. But he was willing."

"I think he was afraid of Hastings."

"Wasn't Maggie?"

"I was always there."

Haddock was as big as Hastings, almost, but the black had twenty years on him.

"Too bad you weren't in the elevator."

For a moment Frye thought Haddock was going to hit him. Thank God he didn't. It would have been like being hit by Roy Hastings.

Three hours later, still in Cassidy's, Haddock long since gone, Frye called Larry Gridiron at home. Maxine answered.

"I thought he was with you."

"He's not home?"

"Where are you calling from?"

"My office," he lied.

"Ha. If you see Larry, send him home."

He dialed Larry's office and got a busy signal. Cassidy's was just across the street from the Arts Building. Frye paid up and left.

The office door was open. Larry sat behind his desk in the inner office, arms folded, eyes closed, apparently fast asleep. The smell of booze was thick in the air. An empty bottle of Black and White was upended in the wastebasket. The phone lay on the desk, complaining loudly. August returned it to its cradle and put his hand on Larry's shoulder in order to rock him awake. Larry tipped and fell over sideways, hitting the floor with a bang.

When August managed to get down beside his old friend, he was filled with foreboding. What had Priscilla said? She took Stanley's pulse and he had none. There was no warmth of breath when he put his hand to Larry's mouth. He was searching around among his chins to find a pulse in Larry's throat when he looked up to see Cable.

"What are you doing, Professor?"

"I think he's dead."

Once, years ago around a table in a room on the fourth

floor of this building, August Frye had been a member of the jury that judged James Branch Cable's performance in his oral exam a failure. He had added his vote to the unanimous decision that Cable be discontinued as a graduate student in English at Lyndon Johnson. When he was told the verdict, James had looked from face to face and for a moment their eyes had locked like this. With the great difference that now Cable was in the role of judge.

"That's two you've found," Cable said. "First Bledsoe, now Gridiron."

Frye was trying to get up from the genuflection he had assumed in order to help his fallen colleague. He put his knee on Larry's chest and began to struggle to his feet. There was a groan.

Dear God, it was Larry. Larry was alive! He looked up wild-eyed at Cable, but the detective was already on the phone.

Terrified but content, August Frye rode in the ambulance with his friend, over whom paramedics from the Third World labored with an air of competence. August Frye's hands were clenched in an attitude of prayer. *Don't let him die*, he prayed. *Don't let him die.*

His orison seemed to radiate outward with the vehicle's flashing lights, then worm its way toward heaven with the wail of the ambulance.

4

MAXINE GRIDIRON WAS CHAIN-SMOKING in the waiting room, half turned away from the other anxious people there. To look at them, to talk with them, would be to acknowledge that this was real, that her husband was in the hospital. August Frye had been infuriatingly unclear on the telephone.

"Just get in a cab and come," he had urged her, over and over.

"Have you called a priest?"

On the way to Twenty-third street, her cab was caught in traffic and she sat thinking of the question she had put to August. A priest? For Larry? Larry thought Unitarianism was going too far. It was herself she had thought of. That was when she took a chance, left the cab in midstreet, dashed to a deli, and bought a pack of cigarettes. Her cab still awaited her, the driver glaring at her.

"I wouldna waited."

Fat chance he would drive off without the fare. She ignored him and lit up a cigarette.

"Hey!" He jabbed a Middle Eastern finger at a card scotch-taped to the yellowish partition between them. "Thank You for Not Smoking."

"You're welcome." She dragged deeply on her cigarette. A priest. It was of herself she had been thinking. A lifetime of neglect, but at the end, magic, magic, she wanted a priest by her bedside, waving her into eternity. It did not seem at all funny. The driver was trying to close the perforated communication panel, unsuccessfully. She directed exhaled smoke at it. Who was this Arab to tell her whether or not she could smoke? They blew up airplanes and took hostages but wouldn't touch tobacco or liquor. She thought of Larry, gasping his last, and burst into tears.

August had been waiting for her outside the hospital. He paid the driver, who had gotten out of the cab and opened all four doors. He was airing it out. Maxine ignored him. The great hulking hospital dwarfed her. August took her arm, and she slumped against him.

"How is he?"

For answer, he squeezed her arm. What a time to realize that he was a widower and she might soon be on the market herself. They went through the revolving doors together, making little baby steps, close as Siamese twins. Honestly. On the way up in the elevator unbidden thoughts of Larry's retirement fund, his insurance, came to her. She burst into tears again. August put his arm around her.

Larry was in Intensive Care. It sounded like hand lotion. He looked like a lab experiment, tubes and bottles and stainless steel, the spouse of her bosom flat on his back on a narrow bed that looked as if it could be driven. The nurse wore a disgusted look.

"This is his wife," August explained.

The nurse's bosom was pneumatic, a quick cubistic sketch in starched white planes.

"What's wrong with him?" Maxine threaded her way among the impediments and looked down at Larry. His mouth was open, spittle running freely from one corner. His eyelids fluttered. Was he breathing? She turned and looked wild-eyed at the nurse.

"He won't be here long," the nurse said with some satisfaction.

Numbed by this announcement, Maxine staggered backward. August led her from the room. At the threshold, she stopped their progress by taking hold of the doorframe. She cast a stricken look at Larry, thinking it might be the last. Continuing down the hall, leaning on August, she was like Niobe, all tears. Seated, she took out a cigarette. August lit it for her, then borrowed one for himself.

"What the hell difference does it make," he said, settling on the cracked plastic cushion beside her, air oozing obscenely from it. She looked at her smoldering cigarette. What difference indeed?

"I should be with Larry."

"You heard the nurse."

"Oh, God, God." She threw herself into August's arms.

After fifteen minutes, he went down the hall again, and Maxine avoided the eyes of her fellow sufferers. She had a premonition of what the wake and funeral would be like. There had been enough of them lately: first poor Stanley Bledsoe, then Maggie Downs. She was telling herself that only over her dead body would Hackis say a word over Larry's remains, when August returned.

"They're taking him upstairs."

She stared at him. And angels tend thee to thy rest?

"Substance Dependence. Ninth floor."

"Substance Dependence?"

"They'll dry him out. He'll be good as new."

"Dry him out!" Her first thought was that it was an embalming process, introduced perhaps to cater to the likes of her cabby. And then she understood. "Larry isn't a drunk."

The dread word came out in a whisper. Of course Larry was a drunk. But so was August Frye, and there he stood, free as the breeze. Maxine said she would wait right where she was. August demurred, she insisted, and after a time he left to see how things were going with Larry. Maxine realized that she felt a bit robbed. Widowhood had seemed right around the corner, and now she had a husband in need of drying out.

When she had lit a fourth cigarette—smoke kept the others in the room at bay—Haddock came. He took a cigarette from her pack and lit it, nodding at her through a cloud.

"You know what Dorothy Parker said?"

"What?"

"The poor son of a bitch."

"Larry's alive. They took him upstairs." She leaned toward the assistant dean. "They're going to dry him out."

"The poor son of a bitch. This time I speak for myself. I thought he had cancer."

"Who told you that?"

Haddock shifted on the whoopee cushion and looked across the room. "I forget."

"It was August Frye, wasn't it?"

"Maybe."

"That would be his idea of a joke."

Haddock wore a multicolored corduroy coat and a plaid shirt with a black leather necktie. It was all Maxine could do not to remove that tie, suggest he wear a plain shirt, or throw away the coat. Maybe both.

"Were you ever married?"

"A long time ago."

She smoked in silence, eyeing him pensively. Jane Austen probably had a line that covered Haddock. No wife would permit a man to dress that like. Maxine was surprised Maggie Downs hadn't taken Haddock in hand. You wouldn't think a man like Haddock would work for a woman. A macho type, all those years in the Coast Guard, yet from all reports he had been a docile and loyal assistant to the dean. Larry had hooted at her suggestion that Haddock must be in love with his boss. It was funny, when you thought of it. From Maggie's point of view.

"Poor Maggie, too," Maxine said gently, putting a hand on Haddock's sleeve. He turned, angry at first, then dropped his eyes and nodded.

"Honestly, I wonder if anyone is safe anywhere."

"Lyndon Johnson is in a pretty rough neighborhood."

"But nothing like this ever happened before."

"No. Mainly, it's been muggings."

"Is that what they think, it was just some mugger?"

"They?"

"The police."

"You'd have to ask them."

They were still talking about Maggie when August returned. That was when she learned August had gotten Larry properly registered when he arrived at the hospital.

"They wouldn't take him out of the ambulance until they knew he was insured. His Blue Cross card was in his wallet."

"Where are his things?"

"Upstairs."

She couldn't put it off forever. Besides, she sensed disapproval in these two friends of Larry. She permitted herself to be escorted to the elevator and upstairs to a ward where Larry lay sleeping. On his back. Which of course meant he would snore. She tried to turn him over but was stopped by a nurse's aide. Black. Male. Very large. To subdue unruly patients? Maxine withdrew from the bedside, conceding authority. She decided to stay when August and Haddock said they must go. She would give them ten minutes before leaving herself. She didn't intend to sit here like a statue next to her sleeping husband. The drunk. She hoped they dried him out good and proper.

"You don't have to stay," August told her, but he might have been testing her.

"Of course I'll stay."

He patted her shoulder. "I won't try to talk you out of it."

The truth was, she very much wanted a drink. This was the time she and Larry always had a martini together. Her expression when she looked at August and Haddock was tragic. They were used to being alone, but she was not.

August gave her a kiss. Haddock, awkward, hesitated, then put out his hand. They shook as if they were betting on something.

5

Haddock SEEMED NO MORE excited by the prospect of going off together than he did, but they shared a cab. August got out first, tried to give Haddock money, and watched with relief as the assistant dean was driven away.

Inside, upstairs, shoes off, he settled in front of the television with a cup of tea and was soon asleep.

The screen was an ectoplasmic blur when he awoke, strangely rested, and there was an annoying hum emanating from the television. He leaned forward and turned it off. He remained tipped forward, as if permitting blood to get more easily to his brain. His mind seemed strangely lucid. He sat back, gripping the arms of his chair, and thought of the recent disturbing events. He decided that he would systematically review it all now that it seemed clear that the Hackises were the explanation of what had happened to Maggie. Once one knew the ending, what led up to it should make more sense.

Stanley, of course, was a special case, self-contained, without relation to the Hackises. If there was guilt to be borne there, August knew on whose shoulders it must fall. There was a sense of satisfaction in acknowledging his own guilt, particularly when no penalty could be forthcoming. Besides, he was making recompense. Hopeless as it was, he

178

continued to mail poems of Stanley's off to the editors of the kind of magazine and journal in which Stanley had aspired to appear. August had little doubt that his departed office mate would have taken a kind of pride in being rejected by the *New Yorker*, the *Hudson Review*, the *Atlantic* and even little *Poetry* magazine out in Chicago, hoary with tradition. Doubtless he would have been a bit disheartened by the impersonal printed rejection slips, but still, someone must have read some portion of at least one of the poems before jamming them back into the stamped self-addressed envelope. Old Mr. Bledsoe and August made a little ceremony out of opening the returned poems. Stanley's father saved all the rejection slips, as if they were correspondence of a high order.

"*Commentary*," the old man said, nodding respectfully as he read that the editors were not presently interested in the enclosed manuscript.

"This one is signed," August cried. Alas, it had been fool's gold. How advanced technology was. The signature looked so real, almost as if the ink were wet. But held on the slant beneath a lamp, it revealed itself to have been printed.

Nothing discouraged old Bledsoe. All these letters arriving for Stanley conferred a posthumous importance on his son. August would have gone on mailing out the poems for that reason alone, to please the old man. But he found himself nursing the irrational hope that some editor would buy one. After all, the *Nor'easter* had. But that had been Stanley in his Henry VIII guise. It was tempting to play that trick again, send off a real poem as Stanley's. August succumbed. The editors of the *New York Review of Books* were impersonally uninterested in the enclosed returned manuscript, which bore a poem by Edna St. Vincent Millay falsely ascribed to Stanley Bledsoe.

Seated fully dressed in his Barcalounger before the dead eye of the television at two-thirty in the morning, his mind clear as a bell, without even the usual annoying ringing in his ears, August felt there was nothing he could not understand. At the moment the universe seemed bound by cause and effect, intelligible. Then why had Stanley Bledsoe met his death by accident while being kidnapped by an illiterate student who wanted to pass his course? But the very irrationality of the event was its meaning. That's how life is. Our projects gang agley as a matter of course. It was irrational to expect life to be rational. He let that thought form slowly in his mind, then contemplated it. He had the exhilarating sensation that finally, after all these years, he had cracked the nut of life. How absurd, for example, that he should be sitting up at this hour pondering recent events, as if to surprise their meaning would add something important to the cosmic inventory. Their meaning was that they were meaningless.

Even as he thought that, he knew he would laugh about it in the morning. It sounded like freshman philosophy. But there *was* no meaning in Stanley Bledsoe's death. He thought of Maggie Downs then, and his existential theory evaporated.

Here at last was a clear case of cause and effect. And the motive was the oldest in the book. The moral? Three's a crowd. Maggie had paid the price for frolicking with Hackis, done in by his jogging wife. . . .

On the wide screen of August Frye's now pellucid mind, Maggie emerged from her office and went to the elevator. Her destination was the basement garage. Cable had suggested that Joyce Hackis might have been waiting in the elevator, strangled Maggie as the car descended, and then slipped away a split second before Larry Gridiron discovered the dead dean. That made no sense. She had not jogged up and down the building, but passed through the garage, apparently as she often had before. But that habit could have acquainted her with one of Maggie's—when she usually left for the day. Of course, Joyce in jogging costume was anonymous, rendered a stranger yet unmenacing by her running clothes. Haddock had seen and recognized her.

Frye's mind caught on the rough edge of Larry lurking about in the basement garage. Larry's explanation of his presence there fit the existential theory: it made no sense. August permitted an imagined Larry to wait by the elevator and spring upon the dean when she emerged. Why? But they all had reasons to throttle the dean. Maggie took it to be her mission in life to be hated by the faculty, as if the prospect of anything like approval from them would disgrace her. So August let it happen, in his mind. The elevator door opened, Maggie emerged, the demented Gridiron pounced and choked the life from her. Then he sounded the alarm, calling attention to the body. . . .

August was shaking his head. But he stopped the movement. Larry had been forced to sound the alarm because of the arrival of Haddock. Of course that was it.

Suddenly, he felt very tired. He must explain all this to Cable in the morning. The clue to it all was Haddock's arrival.

Tired as he was, he could not sleep. After a restless hour in bed, he ran a tub of hot water and sat in a sea of bubbles, ashamed of himself for what he must do to Larry Gridiron. Maxine would never speak to him again. But the true punishment, the burden, his albatross, would be the realization that he had betrayed two old friends, first Stanley, then Larry Gridiron.

Back in bed, he dozed fitfully, coming awake again and again, checking the clock. But it was far too early to telephone Cable.

Just before dawn, he fell into sleep like a parachutist and did not wake again until five minutes of ten in the morning.

6

IN THE PROSECUTOR'S OFFICE, Gilligan, his voice heavy with success, explained to Cable the origin, course, and culmination of the investigation of Hackis that had led to the grand jury finding.

"A woman who worked for him when he was in Congress put us onto Hackis. She ran into him in Montego Bay with a woman she knew was not his wife. Not his first wife, at least. The fact that Hackis avoided her, indeed fled with Maggie Downs in a cab for Runaway Bay, convinced her that her old boss was up to no good. Since in the past he had been up to no good with her, this pricked her interest."

Gilligan went on in this vein. He might have been dictating or addressing a jury. Perhaps he always talked this way. Efforts to hurry him along the path of his narrative proved fruitless. Cable took out cigarettes and, when Gilligan did not object, lit one.

"One woman's resentment set you going?"

Gilligan looked across at Cable. His smile was insincere. "I am proceeding chronologically. But you are not completely wide of the mark."

There had been, it emerged, a young woman in the prosecutor's office named Millicent Jones. She was on leave of absence now, suing the prosecutor for sex discrimination against herself ("Her argument is with God, not with me," Harsch the prosecutor had unwisely said in a preliminary hearing, and now Millicent was determined to drive him from office by getting a multimillion-dollar judgment against Harsch's employer, the State of New York). It was Millicent who saw in Hackis's romp in Jamaica an offense of epic proportions. She was given her head by Harsch, but with Gilligan as moderating principal.

"The rest is history," Gilligan said with satisfaction. "Or it soon will be."

"How is Millicent's case against Harsch going?"

"These things take time."

"Where could I reach her?"

Gilligan was nonplussed. "Why would you want to do that? I can tell you everything you want to know. Not that I know why I should."

When Cable left, he had Millicent's address in the upper sixties. Not where one would expect a lower-echelon member of the prosecutor's office to live. Gilligan himself was astounded. The location of her lodgings was obviously news to him. But then, Gilligan had given no explanation of Millicent Jones's presence in Montego Bay.

Millicent Jones was scarcely more than five feet tall, and she looked up at him as if she carried the burden of the great globe itself.

"If this is about my suit, I won't discuss it."

"It's about Hackis and the Lyndon Johnson campus."

She let him in. He had been screened downstairs in the lobby; Millicent Jones had been called to see if she was expecting him. She had permitted him to come up to the tenth floor, but their initial exchange took place through her scarcely opened door, a security chain in place.

The apartment was a work of art, furniture, carpets, paintings, and decor combining in a statement of quiet affluence. Cable was seated in a rose-colored chair, Millicent settled on a sofa.

"I didn't know the precinct had been brought into the Hackis investigation."

She meant the investigation of his financial and amorous misadventures. The mention of the murder of Maggie Downs got no rise from her. Except to elicit a mordant description of Joyce Hackis.

"She's a new breed, not exactly a backslider, but neither old-fashioned nor a new woman. She gives the appearance of being the latter, but her actions betray her. Imagine tolerating her husband's philandering as if it were a male prerogative!"

"I understand you once worked for him."

"In Washington. Yes. The year after I graduated from Mount Holyoke. It's what decided me to go to law school."

"Was he philandering then?"

She crossed her legs. "He made a play for me."

"Ah."

"That determined me to fight for the rights of women."

"Was he unsuccessful?"

Her pointed chin lifted. "I was. Whether he was or not is beside the point."

"Jamaica gave you your chance for revenge?"

She hesitated only for a moment. "Of course that is how you would see it. I have no objection. But it's not simply the settling of a single account. It symbolizes a far larger struggle."

"I don't think anyone would describe Dean Downs as having been seduced by Hackis."

"Oh, no doubt she is a femme fatale."

"She is the woman you saw him with in Jamaica."

Millicent Jones registered the remark and that was all.

"This is a lovely apartment."

"I am independently wealthy. My mother was the mistress of an extremely successful man. My father. They never married. Both are gone now. And this is mine."

The apartment no longer seemed attractive to Cable. Millicent Jones did not look around her with triumphant possessiveness. She and her old lover Hackis were in different jails.

"Have you talked with Hackis lately?"

"Since Jamaica? No."

"I wonder if he knows you are at the bottom of his troubles."

"We both know what is at the bottom of his troubles." She rose, and Cable did too. "Do you think he killed her?"

"It might have been his wife."

Millicent Jones was furious. She sat him down again, demanding why he wished to punish a woman because of Hackis's many crimes against the female sex.

"Well, a witness put her at the scene where it happened, and he wasn't there. She had motive, as you yourself know."

"Motive! Why blame the woman?"

"Maybe you can understand that better than I can."

"Is that a sexist remark?"

"I hope not." If it was, she would doubtless lodge a complaint against him, maybe even sue the city.

She was staring across the room at a window. "I should have taken care of him long ago, in Washington. Many people would have been spared much, and the city would not have been robbed."

"Taken care of him how?"

She turned and smiled sweetly. "With a breath of scandal. He was a Congressman."

Going down the elevator, Cable could believe that she would have done whatever it took if she had decided to bring down Hackis. Well, she was bringing him down now.

Priscilla's claim to have seen Joyce Hackis at Lyndon Johnson the day Maggie was killed no longer held water. The masseuse at Healthland had been kneading Joyce's flesh when she returned after a short run with a cramp in her legs. There was no way Joyce could have been in the garage around the time Gridiron found the body.

"Are we back to a mugger?" August Frye asked when Cable talked to him on the phone.

Maybe they were. It would be a species of surrender. It would be like ascribing an illness to a virus.

7

AUGUST FRYE HAD LEARNED how to call up on the screen of Stanley Bledsoe's computer in the Bronx apartment the files in which his late colleague had stored his incredible output of verse. Here surely was the dark side of the computer age. Evelyn Waugh had divided writers into three kinds: those who can write but have nothing to say, those with something to say who cannot write, and, finally, those speaking at conferences about the agony of creation. But there was a new class now, that to which Stanley had emphatically belonged. Those who have nothing to say and cannot write, but own a computer.

Ah, the fatal facility with which the late Stanley had filled the waiting screen with lines of more or less equal length, the result having the look of poetry but was never the thing itself.

> My father sits alone at home
> He cannot hear the telephone
> He would not hear an atom bomb
> My father sits alone at home.

Old man Bledsoe breathed heavily over August Frye's shoulder when this gem appeared in green letters on a black background.

"He means you," August said, but of course the old man did not answer. Besides, he was reading the lines half aloud. He began to sniffle. August felt like joining him. How could Stanley have imagined that such terrible stuff deserved to be kept? All day he had dealt with the genuine article or, if not precisely that—after all, he taught a course in popular culture in which Edgar Rice Burroughs figured along with Zane Grey—nonetheless with the high competence of the literarily unambitious. Stanley would not have known Edgar Guest, August wrongly thought. The father did, and it appeared he had read the jingly homespun lines of Guest to little Stanley. Who knows how deep down into the grain of imagination go those first memorized lines, the poet first admired? Bledsoe senior was delighted to learn that Professor Frye knew of Edgar Guest.

> Most any fish can float
> And drift along and dream
> But it takes a real live one
> To swim against the stream

How frightening memory is. The words came trippingly to his tongue. He wrote them down so the old man could read them. Later, seated behind his desk in the office, he pulled the folded paper from his pocket. He typed up the quartet, called it "Carping Criticism," and addressed an envelope to the Biloxi Review. He retitled the lines "Be My Guest" and mailed them. Then he went off to keep a promise he had made to his sleepless self the night before. He had renewed it after talking with Cable. Joyce Hackis was out of the picture. Had she ever really been in it? He stopped by the dean's office but was told Haddock was on the phone. Well, maybe Bob wouldn't have wanted to play detective anyway.

From the first-floor lobby, August took the staircase to the basement garage, down down down. If he kept his eyes on his feet, he grew dizzy. At the bottom of the stairs was a steel door bearing the legend "Garage." He leaned against it,

about to use his full weight to lever it open, when the sound
of someone descending the stairs stopped him.

"August?" It was Haddock, piebald in a mustard-colored
suit, black-and-red checked shirt, and paisley tie.

Frye waited for the dean's assistant to reach him.

"I didn't know you drove," Haddock said.

"Last night I was thinking about Maggie's death and
promised myself I would come down here and try to make
sense out of it."

"You think it makes sense?"

"Maybe not. What do you think of Larry's story?"

"Story?" Haddock grunted as he shouldered the door
open. They stepped into the echoing garage with its sweetly
sick smells of exhaust and oil.

"Something doesn't ring true."

"I was going to slip across the street to Cassidy's for a
drink. Care to come along?"

August shook his head virtuously. "I never break a promise to myself. Now, where do you suppose Larry was standing
when the elevator arrived?"

Haddock made an impatient sound.

"Better yet, tell me exactly what you saw when you got
here."

"When I got here? What do you mean?"

"When you came down and found Larry bending over
Maggie's body."

"Is that what I found?"

"Isn't it?"

"I saw what the guard saw."

"But you thought you saw Joyce Hackis that night, and
she wasn't here." August grew didactic. "Methodic doubt,
Bob, that's what we need. We pool everyone's memories,
playing them off against one another."

Haddock looked around the garage. The sound of traffic
came to them, at once muted and amplified from the street,
the odd horn sounding as if it were only a few feet away, but
the murmuring motors filling the Aeolian cavern of the

garage as if coming from a mythical elsewhere.

"What a creepy place," Frye said.

"Let's do it right, August. Let's start from the very beginning if you want to reconstruct what happened." Haddock spoke with resigned determination. "Come on." He punched the elevator button. "We'll go upstairs and retrace the whole thing."

"Good!" Frye's interest in the thing had been waning fast, but the prospect of a companion in an effort to relive the last minutes of Maggie Downs's life renewed his zest. He no longer felt like the only one at Lyndon Johnson who gave a damn how the dean had died.

The elevator door opened, and Haddock stepped aside for him to enter. The car rocked up the shaft, not at all a smooth ride, but the elevator like everything else at Lyndon Johnson was treated with the contempt public property somehow elicits. Haddock had turned to face him but looked over his head at the back of the car, his eyes vacant, a little frown depressing his brows.

August Frye did not recognize the floor on which he emerged, but Haddock put his arm on his elbow. "Up these stairs, August."

"Higher! I thought we were going to Maggie's office."

"First we go up here. We want to do this right."

There was a flight of stairs, metal, that led to a door with a small window embedded in it. Haddock unlocked it and pushed it open, and they were outside. On the roof. In the open air. August was delighted.

"I've never been up here before." He walked over the gravelly surface, gingerly at first, as if fearful he might sink through into the floor below, but with increasing springiness in his step. His pace slowed as he neared the two-foot-high barrier that rimmed the roof.

"Maggie loved it up here," Haddock said.

"Aha." Then there was a connection with their ostensible project. He wouldn't have cared if there were none. Lyndon Johnson was not a high building as height is gauged in

Manhattan, but it was higher than many of those around it. August leaned over the edge and looked far below at the traffic. A car came out of the garage, its nose poised for a moment, then darted into the traffic. If he looked to his left, he could almost see the building that housed Healthland. Haddock sat on the ledge more or less sidesaddle and looked back across the roof.

"Did she come up here often?"

Haddock looked at him. He shook his head. "Only once that I remember. She reacted the same way you just did. Funny how people can live in a building and never wonder what's above or below. I took her up here."

"When was that?"

"The day she died."

A pigeon fluttered down on the ledge some ten feet away and began to parade importantly. Soon it was joined by another. Male and female? They looked identical to August, but he wasn't a pigeon. Then why did he feel suddenly uneasy?

"She wasn't easy to work for, Augie. I'm not complaining, you understand. Did I ever complain?"

"Not to me."

"Not to anyone. But she could be something. She reminded me of my first wife."

"That bad?" It just slipped out.

Haddock laughed. "Almost. But it's the good things you remember. Isn't that true?"

"You're right."

"So Maggie was a bitch, she was a woman, the kind of woman I understand." There was a rough proprietary tone in Haddock's voice.

"You and Hackis."

"The son of a bitch. Can you tell me what she saw in that boneless bastard?"

It occurred to August that in an oblique way Haddock was declaring his love for Maggie Downs.

"Don't tell me you were jealous of Hackis."

Wrong. All wrong. Haddock took hold of his arm, and for an awful moment August teetered backward. His calves quivered with fear and he sat forward, pressing his feet to the roof. He tried to rise, but Haddock's grip prevented that.

"Why would she go for someone like that?"

Haddock's remark that Maggie had been up here on the roof the day she died took on ominous meaning. August looked toward the door through which they had come onto the roof. The distance between the ledge and the door seemed at once short and impossibly long. He took out his handkerchief and went through the motions of blowing his nose. This freed his arms. Suddenly he pushed away from the ledge and went in an odd staggering gallop toward the doorway, his heart in his throat. He reached it, twisted the knob, and pulled.

Nothing. He pulled again, looking wildly over his shoulder. Haddock still sat on the ledge. He was holding up a key.

"I want to go downstairs," August called to him.

Haddock nodded. "Come back here."

He told himself there was no danger, not from Haddock. He had to stop playing policeman, stop imagining what had happened to Maggie. What had happened had happened, and there wasn't anything he could do about it. Besides, he was turning it into a game. He would not think again the thoughts that had caused him to run in panic from the ledge to the door. If he did not think them they could not be true; wasn't that some sort of principle? If there were a philosopher here, he could ask. *Esse est percipi.* Wasn't that the phrase?

"*Esse est percipi,*" he said, approaching Haddock.

"We sat right here, Maggie and I. She pretended she'd never guessed how I felt about her. A bit of advice, Augie. Never tell a woman she reminds you of your wife."

"I think it was Bishop Berkeley. The eye is a ray gun, creating the world as it sweeps around. Things pop into existence on being seen."

"Sit down, Augie."

"I have acrophobia."

"Is it catching?"

They both laughed. It was like old times, across the street in Cassidy's or having coffee in Chock Full O'Nuts. "Not if you withdraw in time."

"She laughed at me, Augie."

His feet were pushed out before him now, and he leaned forward to contemplate the gravel. "Do you know what I said? 'I love you.' Me. I looked at her soulfully and said, 'I love you.' Bob Haddock to Maggie Downs. If I had just put my arms around her first, it might have been different. But after that pronouncement, all she did was laugh. She turned away, trying to escape, laughing all the while. It was funny, I see that now. I didn't find it funny then."

"Then what?"

"She did what you just did. Ran for the door."

"And you had the key."

"I had the key. I was in control. She wasn't laughing anymore. She was frightened of me. The way you are. What you said about seeing? Fear is like that. It creates what it fears. I didn't want to hurt her."

The key dangled loosely from Haddock's fingers. Would it be possible to snatch the key, run to the door, unlock it . . . To think it was to realize how impossible it was, at least for August Frye.

"She came back to me then. She looked different. She walked right up to me and put her arms around me. I still felt that she was afraid of me, but there she was in my arms. That's when she kneed me."

Just what she would have done, of course. Maggie Downs wasn't likely to think a man could get the better of her.

"God, I can still feel it. But she had to get the key. I was hurting so bad, I let her rifle my pockets."

"She got away?"

Haddock nodded, and August Frye wanted to cry out with relief. Haddock was merely recounting The Most Embarrassing Moment of My Life. The Day I Declared My Love to the

Dean. But Maggie had kneed him in the crotch and gotten away. It was worse that it had happened the day Maggie died, but just a bad memory.

"She got away," Haddock said.

"Bob, I wouldn't tell you what I was thinking there a minute ago."

Haddock smiled encouragingly. "Tell me."

"I thought you were going to tell me you got Maggie up here on the roof and killed her."

Haddock's eyes did not seem to be joining in the smile. He shook his head. "Oh, no. I killed her in the elevator. I held it on the eighth floor and brought it down when I heard her below."

"You killed her?" How prosaic it sounded.

"I hadn't planned to. Not that it makes a damned bit of difference."

"Of course it does! It makes all the difference in the world."

"Only if no one knows I did it."

"You shouldn't have told me, then."

"Don't bullshit me, Augie. I know you figured it out."

Had he? "It's just between us. Maggie can't be brought back."

"You want me to trust you?"

"Of course!"

Haddock shook his head. "You couldn't keep your mouth shut. I know you, Augie. You'd tell Larry. You'd tell the cop, Cable. You couldn't keep it quiet. I spent time in the brig when I was in the Coast Guard. Ten days, officers' hours, no court martial. Ten days. I couldn't take ten hours now."

"I'll keep it quiet, Bob. I promise."

Haddock turned and looked over the ledge. My God! Frye sprang to his feet and started away, but Haddock's hand shot out and gripped his coat and pulled him back. He lost his balance and fell forward, his upper thighs hitting the top of the ledge. Eternity opened before him as he looked down at the street. In that microsecond he could have read even with his deficient eyes the license-plate numbers of the cars moving back and forth, enumerated the pores in the skin of passersby. And then he was pulled back.

He crumpled to the roof, and his knees lifted instinctively to the fetal position. His heart was in his throat. He felt as if he had fallen and was lying on the street, miraculously preserved. He looked up. Haddock was sliding his belt from the loops of his multicolored trousers. His expression was a resigned one, as if this were going to hurt him more than it would August.

Two grown men, one in his fifties, the other far older, in his sixties, playing tag on a rooftop, that is how it might have seemed to an observer looking down on them from the higher buildings several blocks away. August scrambled zigzag away from the ledge—he had to stay away from that if he did nothing else—heading again for the raised structure that housed the top of the stairway. When Haddock came toward him, the belt looped menacingly in one hand, August waited, waited until he could see the assistant dean's bloodshot eyes, and then slipped in the opposite direction, around the stairway structure, using it as trees are used by boys in hide-and-seek. Haddock reversed direction, and so did he. All he had to do was keep this elevation between them. Once Haddock nearly caught his wrist, but he escaped and on opposite sides of the stairway they both laughed, August with hysterical relief, Haddock with who knew what emotions.

Finally, August used an old trick. Keeping the raised structure between them, he backed away across the roof to a lower projection housing the air-conditioning. But before he could get behind it, Haddock peeked around the stairway and saw him. August Frye on his knees watched Haddock come slowly, almost wearily, toward him, the belt dangling from his hand. But then his eyes went beyond this threatening figure to the door of the staircase. *Esse est percipi.* Seeing is believing. He dared not believe his eyes that the door was opening. But it was. And there was James Branch Cable.

The detective paused for a second, then sprinted across the roof to Haddock. The acting dean turned at the sound of the approaching footsteps. For a moment it seemed that he would do something to forestall events, but then he sagged, letting his belt fall to the rooftop. Beyond the air-conditioning unit, August Frye collapsed in relief. Above him, a single pigeon soared awkwardly.

The sound of Cable's shouting brought him to his knees. He turned just in time to see Haddock lumber across the roof to the ledge and go over, diving into air.

8

THE GRAND JURY DID not return an indictment against Gregory Hackis. The president of Lyndon Johnson, trim again because of his constant attendance at Healthland with his wife, appeared before the press, Joyce smiling toothily beside him. He bore no resentment, he assured the representatives of the media, indeed he favored the grand-jury system, as he favored everything else in this great republic of ours. Where else could a lad from humble Nebraska origins become first a member of the Congress of the United States and then go on to the presidency of such an institution as Lyndon Johnson?

Beside August Frye, Priscilla snickered. She was out of uniform. It emerged that she had decided to enroll at Lyndon Johnson.

"With what I know about you guys I should get straight A's."

"How's Roy?"

"That son of a bitch."

Millicent Jones's suit against the prosecutor's office was thrown out, but James Branch Cable did not seem elated by the fact. They sat in Cassidy's, near the window, with a view of the street.

"We would have won our case. Against Haddock."

"What made you suspect him?"

"I might ask you the same thing."

August Frye took refuge in silence. Let Cable think he had come to suspect poor Haddock, then confronted him. Dear God, that awful time on the roof with Haddock intent on murder. Would Haddock have hurled his old friend off the roof as in the end he had hurled himself? Frye shivered. But Cable was answering the question.

"Either Maggie Downs's death was merely random or it wasn't. A mugger would have taken her purse, not her life. Both maybe, but not only the less important one to him. Her purse was lying beside her, remember. I ruled out a random mugger. So who did it? It could have been Hackis, it could have been his driver, it could have been Larry, it could have been you, it could have been Haddock."

"Me!"

"Why not? You stuck your nose in at every opportunity, you're a notorious troublemaker. The problem was, you aren't strong enough."

August Frye looked bleakly at his old student, wishing he could refute that sketch of himself. Does anyone really want to know how he seems to others?

"Haddock was also always on the spot. I'll be honest, Professor Frye. I really wasn't sure he was the one. In any case, it was all circumstantial. But when I looked up and saw the two of you on the roof, when I saw the pure terror in your eyes as you hung over the ledge, everything fell into place."

"Everything but me."

"Haddock landed right over there." Cable was pointing. Frye did not look. The acting dean had landed on a car top, denting the roof, dying instantly. What a way to go. But what way isn't?

Maxine asked him to dinner, and it was like old times, sort of. Larry drank a lot of mineral water, but his eye followed August's glass whenever he lifted it to his lips. It made the preprandial manhattan, the dinner wine, and the

brandy afterward so much tastier. This realization seemed
to underscore the unsavory character traits Cable had enumerated.

"If you want out of the chairmanship, I'll back you,
Larry."

"Out? What are you talking about?" Maxine was alarmed.

"I'm staying as chair," Larry said, sober as a judge.

Haddock's death had been treated simply as suicide by
the press—"Depressed Dean Takes Dive"—and James
Branch Cable let it go. None of the murderers running
around the city free had been connected with the events at
Lyndon Johnson Community College. Gridiron had been
quoted as saying that Haddock had left a great emptiness at
the college. Well, he had left an opening, anyway.

"Maybe you should try for dean, Larry."

"Don't be a smartass, Augie. I have good news for you.
You are the Olive Pettigrew Green winner. A special confer-
ral of the award before the assembled student body. Hackis
will pin it on you at last."

He protested, but he was in a weakened position, from
the drink he had consumed, because of the way he had
behaved this past month. Accepting that meaningless award
was the least he could do.

"You deserve it," Larry said, with an edge to his voice.

What could he do but agree?

It was two days later that a poem of Stanley Bledsoe was
accepted by a financial newsletter published in Hoboken.
August Frye had not realized it was a financial newsletter
when he mailed a sheaf of Stanley's verse to the editor. Old
Bledsoe was ecstatic that his son would be immortalized in
the pages of a newsletter advising its readers how to invest
wisely.

"A species of capital punishment," Frye said, but of course
the old man did not hear. He had noticed the misspelling of
his son's name.

"Edgar Bledsoe?" he croaked.

"What's in a name?" But on the legal pad he wrote that

he would have the name corrected. There wasn't much he could do about the poem itself.

Nomen is the Latin name for name.
No men there are who do not thirst for fame.
Nome in Alaska is an icy burg.
No omen warned the unbombed volk of Hamburg.
Name is the English word for nomen.
No man there is who does not need a woman.

It was, as one might say, a good sample of the poetic achievement of Stanley Bledsoe, may he rest in peace.

If you have enjoyed this book and would like to receive details of other Walker mystery titles, please write to:

Mystery Editor
Walker and Company
720 Fifth Avenue
New York, NY 10019